A GLOVES OFF NOVEL

A FIGHTER'S DESIRE

PART ONE

Doni,
Two is always
better than one!
♥ LPDover

USA TODAY BESTSELLING AUTHOR

L.P. DOVER

Copyright © 2014 by L.P. Dover
Cover design by Regina Wamba of Mae I Design
Edited by Melissa Ringsted
Formatting by JT Formatting

Printed in the United States of America
First Edition: July 2014
Library of Congress Cataloging-in-Publication Data
Dover, L.P.
A Fighter's Desire: Part One (A Gloves Off Novel) – 1st ed
    ISBN - 13: 978-1501081521
    ISBN - 10: 1501081527

1.   A Fighter's Desire—Fiction 2. Fiction—Romance
3.   Fiction—Contemporary Romance

http://**authorlpdoverbooks.com**/

NOTE FROM THE AUTHOR

Hello, lovely readers! I wanted to give you a heads up that *A Fighter's Desire* Parts One and Two are introductory novellas so that you can be introduced to the Gloves Off characters. They need to be read in order and definitely before each main book in the series. Also, just to give you a fair warning there are no happy endings yet, but you will get the satisfaction you crave soon. I love my fighters and I want them to have their happily ever afters more than anything. In their main books they will have their chance to be happy.

The GLOVES OFF series order

PART ONE

Two is always better than one.

WHAT WOULD YOU do if you were given the chance to spend the night with not one, but two fighters? Would you do it? Could you open yourself up to the pleasures they offered and do exactly what they said in order to pass on to the next round?

It was common knowledge that Ryley and Camden Jameson, well-known MMA fighters and identical twins, were just as aggressive and passionate in the bed as they were in the ring. The only problem was that if you didn't pass their test on the first night, then you didn't proceed to the next round. They loved a good fight, and that's what they got when they met Ashleigh Warren.

Ashleigh knew what was going to happen when the twins approached her with a proposition, and needless to say, she knew exactly how to handle them … or so she thought. The rules had changed, and in order to get them both she had to first spend one night with each and last until they were done with her. It was a proposition she couldn't refuse, but she knew it wouldn't be easy to win. However, it was one that she was going to enjoy.

CHAPTER

1

Ryley

"YOU ARE SUCH an asshole!" April screamed, her face blood red with rage. She actually looked kind of cute pissed off, but it wasn't enough to get me to change my mind.

Casually, I lounged back on my bed and smiled, which only infuriated her more. "I never said I wasn't, sweetheart. You knew what you were getting in to when you agreed to stay tonight. I didn't promise you anything."

Huffing, she yanked her little red dress over her mussed up blonde hair and smoothed it down her body before marching toward the door. "Yeah, but I didn't think you were going to turn into an inconsiderate douche bag either."

"Yeah, well I'd like to hear you say that to the next

guy you almost castrate. Seriously, I'm doing both of us a favor. You might want to practice sucking dick without using your fucking teeth."

She scoffed and threw open the door, only to come face to face with my twin brother, Camden, who was the exact replica of me. He was shirtless, wearing a pair of jeans with the biggest grin on his face and his hand up in the air about to knock. If he was at my door that meant his date wasn't any better.

"Everything okay in here?" he asked teasingly, gazing up and down her body.

"Ugh ... fuck you," she snarled, glancing back and forth at us. "Fuck you, both."

Pushing her way past Camden, she stormed down the hallway, her thunderous footsteps echoing until I heard the front door open and slam shut. "Dude, what the hell happened?" he asked, bursting out in laughter. "You two were basically getting it on in the living room just a few minutes ago."

"Oh, I know. It was fun until she decided to go down on me. The bitch seriously needs to learn how to suck a dick. I swear, I thought she was going to bite the fucking thing off."

Camden cringed. "Ouch! Well, I'm glad I didn't pick *her* tonight. Although, I can't say my choice is much better."

Chuckling, I slipped out of bed and pulled on a pair of jeans. After the party tonight, we'd both made our picks on who we wanted; he chose a long-legged brunette while I picked April, a petite and curvy blonde.

"Oh yeah, and why is that?" I asked.

Camden groaned and shut my door, talking low so his

date couldn't hear him. "The girl can't kiss for shit. It's like I'm drowning each time she opens her mouth. Why is it so hard to find a girl who knows what she's doing?"

That was a good question. If there was one thing I loved doing, it was fighting and fucking. I delighted in being with women, enjoying different varieties, and appreciated them even more when they knew how to get me off. I didn't want someone inexperienced, but I also didn't want a whore.

Camden and I wanted someone who was in between; someone who knew what she was doing and who hadn't been with a shit ton of men. Unfortunately, it was hard to find a woman like that.

"I don't know, but I'm sure as hell going to find one. We need someone different, someone who's not part of our crowd," I said, answering my brother's question.

With a mischievous smirk on his face, Camden nodded and opened the door. "I agree. Well how about we go and find us one? I can sacrifice a night to go out."

Camden and I had strict rules during fighting season, so we kept to our coach's rules and abstained from sex right before our fights. It just so happened that our next fight was the last one for a couple of weeks. I was going to make sure I enjoyed that time off, too.

Grabbing a shirt from my closet, I slipped it over my head and clapped my brother on the shoulder. We were completely identical, except I had a small scar at my hairline above my left eye, which always gave my identity away. Therefore, to keep people from telling us apart, we always wore baseball caps so I could hide it.

"Let's go then," I told him. "Ditch your girl and we'll get the hell out of here."

I wanted to have some fun.

CHAPTER 2

Ryley

CRAVING SPEED, CAMDEN and I hopped on our motorcycles and headed down to Cloud Nine, which was one of the most popular clubs in all of downtown Los Angeles. When we pulled up to the club, the valet guys recognized us and pointed to the valet parking deck so that we could park our bikes. The one good thing about being VIP members was that we got treated like royalty.

I fucking loved it.

"Dude, you kicked ass last weekend," one of the valet guys shouted. From this distance, I could tell by the shaved head, tattoos on both arms, and short, stocky stature that it was Andres, one of the club bouncers.

Taking off my helmet, I strapped it to my bike and shook his outstretched hand. "Thanks, man. It was a good fight. So how is it in there?" I asked, nodding toward the club.

Andres chuckled and slapped me on the back. "It's wild, but I know you boys are used to that. Come on, I'll let you go in through the back. That way no one gets pissed."

"Hell yeah," Camden retorted. "The last thing we need is to get arrested again, or we'll be kissing the championship good-bye."

At another club downtown last week, Camden was provoked by a random guy who thought he could best him. Unfortunately, Camden had a few drinks in his system and kicked the guy's ass. The fucker pressed charges, but they were eventually dropped since witnesses claimed Camden was taunted.

He got lucky, even though we both knew he was guilty as hell. Walking away from a fight wasn't something we were good at. It was in our blood … in our hearts. Fighting was all we knew. Well, that and screwing around with women. It was what we lived for, what we wanted.

Andres led us to the side of the building, where another bouncer stood watch in case someone tried to sneak in. Both guys were huge, more along the lines of a linebacker with their hulking frames and muscles as big as my thighs. I was a big guy, but they put me to shame.

As soon as we walked in, Andres led us through the throng of people. When we got to the bar, he tapped his hand on the counter to get the bartender's attention. "Stay out of trouble, boys. Enjoy yourselves."

"Take care, man," I said, bumping his fist. "And thanks for letting us in the back."

Nodding, he turned and called out over his shoulder,

"No problem."

Once he left, it was time to party. "What's up, guys, you having the usual tonight?" the bartender asked.

His name was Eric, but on some nights he went by Erica, depending on which bar he was working at. The strange thing about him was that he wasn't gay. He had long, brown hair just past his shoulders and a small frame, very feminine, and he had a girlfriend who was hot as shit. She didn't seem to mind his wardrobe changes though. In fact, she seemed to love it which never made any sense to me.

Since Camden was too busy scanning the crowd, I ordered for us. "Yeah, I'll have a gin and tonic, and make Cam his usual rum and Coke."

As soon as he finished the drinks, Camden gulped his down and set the empty glass on the bar, keeping his gaze on a group of girls grinding against each other on the dance floor.

His grin grew wider as he elbowed me in the side. "I think that has my name all over it, brother. Are you going to join me?"

The girls were hot, but they weren't what I was looking for. All three were blonde, and I'd already been jaded by one tonight; I wanted a sultry brunette. Grabbing a seat at the bar, I took another sip of my drink and waved him off. "No, you go ahead. I'll find what I'm looking for later."

"Suit yourself. It means more for me."

Not wasting any time, Camden joined the group of girls and they surrounded him, rubbing their hands and bodies all over him. *He's definitely going to get some ass tonight.* It wasn't long before they slowly started to sidle off the dance floor, heading to the back of the club. They were going straight to the VIP rooms.

"You want another one?" Eric asked, taking away my empty glass.

About that time, a hand brushed across my shoulders. I glanced up to find exactly what I'd been looking for … a sultry brunette with eyes the color of honey. *Oh yeah, just what I wanted.*

Dressed in a skin tight red dress, I couldn't help but gaze down her curvy body. When she noticed me looking, she poked out her chest a little more, showing off the swell of her nipples, which poked out of the fabric. It was like they were beckoning me, inviting me to take them into my mouth. I licked my lips in response, knowing very well I was going to have them soon.

Smiling, she bit her lip and murmured in my ear, "Can I buy you a drink?"

She took my hand and placed it on her hip, slowly trailing it over her ass. I squeezed and brought her closer, and in return she grazed her hand along my thigh and over my cock.

"How can I refuse?" I replied, noting that she wasn't wearing any underwear.

Good, I could drag her away and fuck her, quickly and easily. My dick was getting hard just thinking about it.

I nodded to the bartender and smiled, fixing up another gin and tonic before pouring it into a glass. Turning to the dark-haired beauty, I smiled and held it up. "Thank you for the drink. What's your name? I'm Ryley."

Grinning, she watched my mouth as I took a sip of my drink. "Oh I know who you are," she murmured heatedly. "I think every woman in this place knows who you and your brother are. I just happened to get lucky enough to spot you first." She held out her hand. "I'm Megan."

I chugged the rest of my drink and took her hand. "Well, Megan, how about we go out on the dance floor and you show me your moves?"

Pressing her body to mine, she chuckled low. "Or better yet," she whispered in my ear, "how about you show me yours?" Her hand grazed down my chest to the button on my jeans. "How does that sound?"

"Lead the way, baby."

As we danced our way through the crowd to the back rooms, my dick got harder with each step. Since April— the castrator—didn't finish the job earlier, I needed the release. Once we were hidden away in a dark corner of a VIP room, she wrapped her arms around my neck and I grabbed her ass, lifting her up so she could fold her legs around me.

"I'm surprised you didn't want to talk first," I teased, reaching into my back pocket for a condom. I always carried a couple with me everywhere I went.

Megan moaned, licking her lips. "Talking's overrated, don't you think?"

"That it is," I agreed.

With one hand, I unzipped my pants and pulled out my cock before tearing open the condom wrapper with my teeth. After sliding it down over me, I lifted her dress up above her waist and pushed her harder into the wall, making her moan.

No one was around, and even if they were, my body shielded hers since she was smaller and more petite. Besides, everyone knew to leave me alone if I was in my zone.

Reaching behind her, I circled my finger between her legs and groaned at how wet she was. I pushed two fingers inside of her and felt her clench tight, drawing me in. "Oh yeah, you're ready for me, aren't you?"

Moaning, she lowered the top to her dress and played with one of her nipples, making it perk up even more. "You have no idea how ready I am."

Lowering my lips, I pulled her nipple into my mouth and sucked hard, biting down so I could hear her scream. The music in the other room muffled any noise that came from these separate rooms, so I didn't have to worry about anyone hearing. In fact, her strangled cry of ecstasy only made me want to hear it again … so I bit down even harder.

Unfortunately, her scream wasn't the only sound I heard …

"Bitch, what the fuck are you doing?" a guy shouted from behind.

Megan tensed in my hold and gasped, immediately letting her legs fall away from my waist, obviously terrified. Before turning around, I slid off the condom and threw it on the floor, buttoning up my jeans. However, I didn't expect what happened next.

The second I turned around, my jaw cracked and lit up like fire. The prick behind me had punched the shit out of my face. My head snapped to the side, but being the trained fighter I was I corrected myself just as quickly and went into fight mode. The taste of blood slid down my throat and my cheek throbbed from biting into it.

This motherfucker's going to pay for that.

The guy was a little taller than me—and stockier—but he was sloppy and drunk. Before I could land a hit,

Megan tried to reason with him. Suddenly, he slapped her before pushing her so hard into the wall that she fell to the floor.

"What the fuck?" I growled angrily, seeing only red as Megan shakily got to her feet.

That's it ... this guy is done. I wasn't in the ring; I was dealing with a douche bag that got off on hitting women. He needed to be put in his place.

Charging toward him, I tackled him to the floor and pummeled his face, over and over with my fists. My knuckles started to tear open and bleed, but I didn't care; I wanted him to hurt. He had two friends with him who tried to pull me away, but after I punched one and felt his nose crack, they both backed off and left the room.

Blood was everywhere ... on my hands, my clothes, and all over the floor as the fucker beneath me coughed, spitting out two of his teeth. I wanted to break his face until they all came out.

Megan's scream, however, was what drew me out of my zone.

"Ryley, please stop!" she cried. "Oh my God, please."

Teeth clenched and breathing hard, I was ready to kill, but I stopped and immediately pulled away, getting to my feet. About that time, Andres burst into the room followed by more bouncers and two police officers.

Great, I thought. *I'm fucked.*

Andres and one of the officers went straight to the guy on the floor. Meanwhile, the other officer approached me head on. I knew the drill all too well, so I placed my hands behind my head, not even resisting when he cuffed me. By the look in his eyes, he'd been prepared for a fight, but I knew better than to do that.

The last thing I wanted was to be banned from the UFC, and knowing my luck I was probably going to be after what I'd done. I may have hit the cocksucker one too many times, but he deserved it.

"Care to tell me what's going on, son?" the officer asked.

He was older, probably in his early fifties, and most likely ex-military judging by the dog tags around his neck and the buzz cut; very authoritative looking and almost the exact image of my father.

My father was my biggest supporter and the one who inspired my brother and me to fight. He passed away two years ago after a motorcycle accident, and ever since then nothing had been the same. I may be spending the night in jail, but he would've done the same thing if he saw a man hit a woman.

Since the guy on the ground was knocked out, I knew I was going to be the guilty party no matter what I said. Thankfully, Megan spoke up on my behalf. Gone was the girl who seduced me, and in her place was a scared woman, terrified.

"It wasn't his fault, Officer, it was mine," she cried, her voice shaking.

"And how is that?" the officer asked, turning his attention to her. Swallowing hard, she looked down at the guy on the floor and then sheepishly at me. She briefly closed her eyes before turning toward the officer. It didn't take a genius to figure it out … the son of a bitch was her boyfriend.

"My boyfriend caught me in here with Ryley, sir. When he found us, he made the first move and hit Ryley. It was stupid of me, and I shouldn't have done it. I promise, Ryley was only defending himself."

"And you," I added angrily, glaring at her. "I was defending you. Why would you want to be with someone who hits you like that? Has he done it before?"

Shrugging, she once again closed her eyes and sighed. "Not really. I mean, he's only done it two times."

The officer held up his hand, signaling for us to stop. "Okay, hold up," he said, turning to Megan. "Did that guy hit you tonight?"

Wrapping her arms around her stomach, she wearily nodded her head. "Yes, he slapped me and pushed me into the wall. After that, Ryley started to fight him. It's not Ryley's fault," she pleaded again.

"That may be true, but I still need to take him to the station until your boyfriend wakes up. They're both coming with me."

The officer read me my rights and we followed Andres through the back to the squad car. I was put in one and dickhead was put in the other, still passed out. Nervously, Megan came over to the car I was in and leaned down toward the window.

"I'm so sorry about this," she cried. "I never meant for any of this to happen."

"Yeah, well, next time don't try to fuck someone else when you have a boyfriend," I growled.

She averted her gaze and closed her eyes. "I know. It was wrong of me. I guess it just felt like freedom to get away from him. I don't even know how he found out I was at Cloud Nine."

The officer finally got into the car and glared back at us. "Okay, miss, it's time to wrap it up. Say your goodbyes."

"Look," I said, "I don't know you very well, and I'll admit, I don't treat girls the way I should, but I *do* know that none of them deserve to be hit. You need to get away from him."

She nodded, tears streaming down her face when she opened her eyes. "I will. Is there anyone I need to call for you?"

Camden was still inside having the time of his life while I was bloody and confined in a police car. "Yeah, I need you to find my brother. He's in the club somewhere. You can't miss him because he looks just like me."

"Oh, I know. I've seen you two in the ring. I'll go find him for you and let him know what's going on."

Turning on her heel, she ambled off toward the back door of the club. "Megan!" I shouted.

She wiped her eyes and turned around hesitantly. "Yeah?"

As much as I should hate her for putting me in the position I was in, I couldn't help but realize there was a larger problem at hand. "On Monday night, meet me at the gym on Sykes Street."

"Why?" she asked skeptically, furrowing her brows.

The officer put the car in gear and slowly started moving out of the parking lot. "Because I'm going to teach you how to defend yourself." Before he could roll up the window, I shouted, "Meet me there at seven!"

Her reply came instantly. "I'll be there!"

CHAPTER 8

Ryley

AFTER SITTING AT the station for four hours twiddling my fucking thumbs, I figured my brother would at some point come to get me. I called and texted, but nothing. At least I was free to go with no charges against me. *Thank God.*

"Is there anyone else you can call?" the officer asked. "Your family? A friend? Your coach?"

The officer's name was Brigg and I was right when I thought he was ex-military. For the past couple of hours he'd told me stories of his time overseas, and it just so happened that he and my father were both at Camp Pendleton during the same time frame.

Unfortunately, I definitely couldn't call my coach. He had already threatened to leave me and my brother behind if we got into any more trouble. My mother was out of the question; in her eyes, my brother and I never got into any trouble. It would crush her to know what we were really like, especially since it was after my father's death when things started to change.

There was only one other person who I knew wouldn't judge me. She wouldn't judge me, but she sure as hell was going to be pissed at me for calling her at three in the morning.

"Actually, there is," I said, reaching for my phone. Once I found her number, I bit my lip and dialed.

Her voice was groggy when she answered, but it didn't stop the giggle that escaped her lips. "Let me guess, Ryley, you figured out that you're in love with me and you couldn't wait to tell me, so you called at," I could hear the rustle of her sheets as she turned in bed, "three in the morning. Geez, couldn't you wait for another few hours?"

I chuckled. If she wasn't off limits I would've tried to get with her. Unfortunately, that would never be possible considering her brother was one of my friends and threatened to kick anyone's ass that messed with her. I wasn't about to go head to head with Matt 'The Destroyer' Reynolds.

"I wish that were true, babe, but I need your help. Can you come pick me up from the police station?"

"Oh my God, you got arrested?" she squealed incredulously. "What the hell did you do?"

Sighing, I looked down at my hands which were split open, but thankfully, no longer bloody. "It's a long story, Gabby. Is there any way you can come get me?"

She huffed and I could hear her getting out of bed. "Fine, I'll be there in about thirty minutes. You owe me,

Ryley."

She had no idea.

Thirty minutes later, Gabriella Reynolds walked through the door in a pair of pink pajama pants and a CSU sweatshirt, her long, midnight-colored hair pulled up in a ponytail. She was a good friend, and probably the only female I could say that about.

When her gaze landed on me, she covered her mouth with her hand and laughed. "Wow, I must say ... you sure know how to party. Do you ever do anything other than fight?"

A mischievous grin spread across my face. "Do you really need me to answer that?"

Holding her hands up, she rolled her eyes and scoffed. "Okay, never mind. I already know what you and your brother like to do. Now come on and let's go so I can get your worthless ass home."

Putting my arm around her shoulder, I squeezed her tight and bent down to kiss her cheek. "What would I do without you, Gabby? Thank you for coming to get to me."

"Oh, it doesn't come without a price, Mr. Jameson. There's something I want from you."

We ventured out into the parking lot and stopped by her little silver sports car. She turned to face me with a sly smile, folding her arms across her chest. I knew that look; she was up to something. "Why do I get the feeling I'm going to regret this?" I asked.

"I wouldn't necessarily say you'd regret it, but it is going to take some work."

"What do you want?"

Her grin grew wider. "You have a fight next weekend, right?"

"Yeah."

"And of course afterwards there'll be a party?"

Sighing, I stared at her hopeful gaze, knowing very well what she wanted, and nodded. "Yes, but you know you can't go to it. Your brother would kick my ass. He already hates the fact that we hang out together."

"Tell me about it," she groaned. "He just knows how you and your brother are. What he fails to realize is that I'm a grown woman and can make my own decisions."

She was a grown woman all right. She was fucking hot and a newbie fighter as well. Her brother had been teaching her mixed martial arts for a while, and I helped her fight every now and again; she was a firecracker in the ring.

"So why are you wanting to go to this party? What's in it for you?"

She winked and bit her lip. "I have my own reasons, Ryley. Get me into the party and I'll call everything even."

"How about you bring a friend and then we'll call it even," I countered. "I'd love to meet one of them. How about your friend Ashleigh? You always talk about her."

Gabriella rolled her eyes. "Yeah, I'm not going to let you seduce my friend. Besides, I don't think she'd fall for your schemes. She's a smart girl and definitely not someone to play around with."

"So basically what you're saying is that she can't

handle me, is that it?" I asked, chuckling.

Laughing, Gabriella strolled over to her side of the car. "Oh, Ryley, if only that were true. I hate to say this, but it's the other way around … *you* wouldn't be able to handle *her*. Not even with the help of your brother."

I scoffed. "Yeah, right. I have yet to find a female I couldn't handle. You have no idea what I can do in the bedroom."

She nodded. "True, but I've heard plenty of stories about you and your brother's trysts in the bedroom. I must say it's pretty interesting. You know, one of these days you're going to want to stop doing that and settle down with *one* woman."

"I'm not a one woman kind of guy, sweetheart. There's too many to pick just one."

Gabby held up her hands up in defeat. "Okay, fine, have it your way. I'll bring Ashleigh, but don't say I didn't warn you."

Getting in the car, I looked over at her and smiled. "Then I'll get you into the party. Leave your brother to me."

I loved a good challenge.

CHAPTER 4

Ryley

MONDAY ROLLED AROUND and it was time to get back to work, to training. Camden apologized for not picking me up at the police station, and like I already knew, it was because he was busy fucking the three girls at the club. At least someone had fun. Thankfully, my motorcycle was still there in the parking lot when we went back to pick it up.

When we walked into the gym, I saw the owner, Carter Bennett—who also happened to be Gabriella's brother's coach—down at the ring talking to mine, Danny Echols. Carter was probably somewhere in his late forties and a head shorter than my coach by almost a foot, but he was one of the most hardcore fighters I knew.

Gabriella's brother definitely had one of the best

coaches around along with me. My coach was a little bit older, but he was just as bad ass as Carter. Thankfully, my brother and I were early which earned us an appreciative smile from him when we approached. I had to make sure he didn't find out about last night.

Matt Reynolds was in the ring, battling it out with Mason Bradley, two of the best Heavyweight UFC fighters of my time and also my mentors. "You better train hard this week, brother," Camden commented. "You're up against Nate Anderson this Saturday."

I sneered at him. "Please, I'm not worried about that fucker."

"Okay," he chuckled. "I'm just saying the guy's gotten better. I've been watching his fights."

So have I and I knew I could take him. "I'm not going to lose, I can promise you that."

After setting our gym bags down, Danny nodded at us and hopped into the ring, putting on his black gloves and headgear. Danny was a retired MMA fighter just like my father had been, and also one of his good friends.

When my father died, Danny took up the role as coach and made sure to push us hard, to make us better. He was a Heavyweight fighter when he fought and even to this day he still kept up the muscle mass; it was impressive. His salt and peppered hair, however, hadn't kept up with the times so he kept it shaved close to his head so no one would be able to tell it was thinning.

"Let's go, boys," he commanded. "We've got lots of work to do."

Every day of training, Camden and I practiced with Danny, and the rest of the time we fought against each other. We always anticipated each other's next steps, making it hard to ever surprise the other in an attack. When the time came for me to fight him in the ring, it was going to be one interesting battle.

Camden elbowed me in the side as I was putting on my gloves. "Hey, some of the guys are going out for drinks tonight. You want to go?"

"What time?" I asked.

"Around seven I think."

I sighed. "I can't. I'll be busy."

"All right, but if you change your mind we're meeting at Bailey's Bar."

I had plans to teach Megan some self-defense moves—if she even decided to show—but if she stayed with her cocksucker boyfriend I knew she'd bail on me. I wished everyone had self-defense training. If Carter allowed it, I'd enjoy teaching a couple of classes every now and again. Knowing how to defend yourself was important; it could save your life.

Three years ago, Camden and I had shown some defense moves to our cousin, Emery, who had just graduated high school and was about to go away to college. Those moves helped her fight off an attacker one night as she was walking back to her dorm.

The guy had raped three girls during that month and she would've been the fourth if she hadn't used the moves we taught her. Luckily, the campus security apprehended him as he tried to stumble away. If I was there I would've killed him.

"Well, if it isn't the twins of terror," Matt teased, leaning over the ropes. "Why don't you boys get up here and let the professionals show you how to fight?" He had the same dark hair and green eyes as Gabriella, and both of them liked to joke around. It was uncanny how they were so much alike.

I smiled up at him and flexed my muscles. "You know I would, but I'm afraid I'll hurt you. We can't have that now can we?"

Matt hopped out of the ring while Camden jumped up, getting in with Mason and our coach. While they sparred back and forth a bit, I figured it would be the best time to get Matt's approval for Gabriella.

"Are you ready for your fight this Saturday?" I asked him.

He grabbed his water and chugged it down before replying, "Yeah, are you?"

"You know it. Hey, listen, I need to ask a favor."

Setting his empty bottle down, he chuckled and wiped the sweat off of his face with a small, dark blue towel. "Uh oh, I don't think I've ever heard that come out of your mouth. I'm almost scared to know."

"Well, it has to do with your sister."

That definitely got his attention. Pursing his lips, he immediately crossed his arms at his chest and glared at me.

Holding up my hands, I quickly said, "Dude, it's not what you think. She picked me up from the station last night after I got into a fight at Cloud Nine. I owe her, and her request was that I talk you into letting her come to the party this Saturday after the fight."

Matt groaned and shook his head. "I can't believe she asked for that. She knows I don't like her going to the parties. I realize what happens at them."

"Yeah, but she's a big girl, too. Everyone understands that they need to keep their distance from her. You probably need to loosen up on her … if you don't, she's likely to rebel and start fucking every single fighter she can. I'm pretty sure you don't want that."

"Hell no I don't," he growled, sounding defeated. Sighing, he sat down on one of the workout benches and started taking off his gloves. "But I guess you also have a point. If I let her go, I need you to promise me you'll keep your eye on her. I'll talk to Tyler and make sure he watches out for her as well."

"And if I promise you'll let her come?"

Reluctantly, Matt nodded in reply.

"All right, I promise then. Do you want me to call and tell her the good news, or will you?"

Taking out his phone, he shook his head. "I'll do it. I need to talk to her anyway and ask her when she wants to meet for another training session."

Matt clapped me on the shoulder and walked away to call Gabriella. Now all I had to do was make sure she didn't get into any trouble at my party.

It was six-thirty and everyone had already left, including Camden and my coach. "You trying to get some extra workouts in or something?" Carter asked after training.

"No," I told him. "I'm meeting someone here at seven. I'm going to teach her some self-defense moves."

Carter laughed. "Ah, is that what you call it these days?"

I set up my weights on the straight bar and smiled up at him before turning serious. "It's actually not like that this time. This girl really needs help and I'm going to give it to her."

"Is everything okay?" he asked curiously.

Sighing, I shrugged my shoulders and sat down on the bench. "Have you ever thought about having someone teach self-defense classes here?"

He nodded. "At one time I did, but all of the people who are qualified to do it already have too much on their plate. No one has the time."

"I'll do it," I answered in all seriousness. "Two nights a week after I train I'll do it if you'll just advertise it."

Dumbfounded, Carter stared at me with wide eyes. "Why is this so important to you? I've never seen you this fired up over anything other than kicking someone's ass."

My cousin came to mind, as did Megan. "It just is," I replied. "I think everyone should know the basics on how to protect themselves."

Carter smiled and patted me on the shoulder. "Okay, I'll get it set up. You can start next week."

As soon as he walked off, Megan came strolling through the door wearing a pair of tight black shorts and a pink tank top, her chocolate brown hair in a high ponytail. Her face was clear of any makeup, and I realized she was much more beautiful without it.

I hardly ever saw women without all of that shit on their faces, so it was hard to get an idea of what lied beneath. She looked innocent ... and completely vulnerable; a prime target for cocksuckers like her boyfriend.

When she saw me, she smiled sheepishly and waved before walking over. "Hey," she greeted. "I'm a little early, I hope that's okay."

"No, it's perfectly fine," I said, getting to my feet. "Let's get you ready." She followed me into the ring and sat down on the mat, mirroring my stretches.

"I want to thank you for doing this, Ryley. And just so you know, I broke up with Alex yesterday. I should have done it a long time ago."

"Well, at least you've done it now. No woman should have to put up with that. Starting next week I'm going to teach self-defense classes for two nights. Why don't you sign up?"

After we stretched and I helped her up from the mat, she looked up at me with her tear-filled honey eyes. "I'd like that," she whispered, her lip trembling. "Where do I sign up?"

"Right here," Carter called out, holding a clipboard. "The class will be available on Tuesday and Thursday nights. You're his first student."

Wiping away her tears, she laughed it off and took the clipboard, signing her name under both days. As soon as she handed it back to Carter and he walked away, she turned to me, determination evident on her face.

"All right, let's see what you've got. Turn me into a fighter, Ryley. I refuse to be a victim anymore."

"Then let's get to it."

CHAPTER 5

Ashleigh

THE WEEK FLEW by because of midterm exams, which were most likely going to kill me before I even finished them. I probably drank enough coffee and other caffeinated drinks to last me a lifetime.

Thankfully, once I turned in my paper to my Marine Biochemistry teacher I wouldn't have to worry about any more tests for another few weeks. *Thank God*. The first thing I was going to do when I went back to my apartment was sleep for a whole twenty-four hours.

Only one more question to go on this exam and I'd be done.

Once I scribbled in my answer, I breathed a sigh of relief and sat back in my chair. Half of the class was still in the room, including Gabriella who was giddy with excitement. She was my best friend and roommate, and tomorrow night we were going to celebrate by going to a party ... and it wasn't just a normal party, either. Her brother, Matt Reynolds, was a famous UFC fighter, and for the first time ever he'd given her permission to go to one of the after parties.

Gabriella had wanted to go for so long, but her brother was afraid she'd get caught up and hurt by one of the fighters. What he didn't understand was that it was *her* who would most likely hurt them ... literally.

A couple of days a week, her brother trained her in the art of fighting, and now she was a kick ass fighter. I trained with her one time, and when I left with a bloody nose I vowed to never do it again.

Still, even with all of her fighting skills, Matt would always be the overprotective older brother that she loved and adored. Unfortunately, fighting couldn't protect the heart.

After packing up my books, I grabbed my exam paper and tentatively walked up to the professor's desk. With a deep breath, I slowly held it out to her; in return, she glanced up at me, smiling. "Stop stressing, Ashleigh. I'm almost positive you passed it after all of the studying you've done," she whispered low.

"I know, but I can't help it."

"I understand. I was the same way when I was your age," she explained, nodding toward the door. "Now go and enjoy your weekend."

"Yes, ma'am."

As soon as I opened the door, I saw my friend Colin, leaning against the wall with a grin on his face. "It's about time you got done with that exam. I swear I thought I was going to have to wait the full two hours on you."

Dressed in his green and white baseball uniform, his hat covering the stark blond hair of his head, I had to admit he was sexy as hell watching me with those bright green eyes of his. Unfortunately, he was just my friend since he had a girlfriend back in his Seattle hometown. He was also my lab partner and had been for the past three years.

"Oh, stop whining," I teased. "You didn't have to wait on me."

"Well, I thought we could eat lunch together before I leave for the weekend. Our tournament starts tomorrow, so Bradley and I will be gone until Sunday night. He wants to see Gabriella before we go."

I chuckled. "That's no surprise. Is he meeting us here?"

"No, he said he would meet us at the café."

There was a small café on campus that had the best panini sandwiches ever. If we didn't eat lunch in our favorite spot on campus by the huge black oak tree, we'd always eat in the café. I was going to miss it when I graduated.

"I swear if they don't get together soon I don't know what I'm going to do. I've never seen two people play so hard to get like they do," I complained.

"Tell me about it. He annoys the fuck out of me every day about her."

We both chuckled and sat down on the bench in the hallway while we waited for Gabriella to get done with her exam. "She should be done soon. You don't mind if we wait on her, do you?"

Taking my bag, he set it on the floor and shook his head. "No, not at all. So what are your plans this weekend?"

"Gabriella and I are going to watch her brother's fight tomorrow night, and then we're going to the after party."

Colin furrowed his brows. "I thought she wasn't allowed to go."

"Well, apparently she bailed one of them out of jail or something on Saturday night, and for payment she asked him to work his magic on her brother. It worked because he called her the other day and said she could go."

"And you're going, too?"

"Yeah, she promised her friend she would bring me. I kind of *have* to go."

His gaze darkened, but before he could say anything in response, Gabriella burst through the door. "Thank God, it's over," she breathed. "I'm starving."

"Well, that's why we we're waiting on you," I chimed. "Colin and Bradley want to eat lunch before they leave. Bradley's going to meet us in the café."

"Sounds good to me." She sauntered off ahead of us and we followed, but Colin gently took my elbow, holding me back.

"What's wrong, are you okay?" I asked.

His gaze was heated, full of concern. "You're not going to hook up with any of those guys at that party are you?"

Incredulously, I laughed and linked my arm with his. "Colin, don't worry about me. I'm a big girl."

"You didn't answer my question. I don't want you getting in over your head."

"I'm not going to. Besides, I'm single and in college. I think I'm entitled to get a little wild and crazy every once in a while. I was fine when we went to the beach, wasn't

I?"

He sighed. "Yeah, but you had me there with you. I looked after you."

Stopping mid-step, I circled around in front of him and put a hand to his chest. I swear if he didn't have a girlfriend he would be the perfect guy to be with. He was funny, smart, sexy as hell, and had the most gorgeous green eyes I'd ever seen. However, he was my friend and that was all it ever would be.

"I know you looked after me, Colin, and you have no idea how much I appreciate it. You're a good friend. Your girlfriend is one lucky lady. Maybe one day I'll find a guy just like you. However … in the meantime I'm going to enjoy the time I have. So whatever happens with me, you don't have to worry, okay? I know what I'm doing."

He blew out a frustrated breath and nodded. "Okay, I believe you. Just make sure you call me if you need me."

I kissed him on the cheek. "Don't I always?"

CHAPTER 6

Ashleigh

"ASHLEIGH, SO HELP me God if you don't get your ass out of that room I'm going to burn every single one of your books! I don't want to be late!"

Gabriella and I were both studying Marine Biology at California State University and heading into our final year before graduation. Ever since I'd met her in our Marine Ecology class, we'd become good friends.

Eventually, we rented an apartment together so we could get out of the dorms. Burning my books wouldn't be good because I needed them, unlike her who never had to open one to pass a test.

Gabriella's thunderous footsteps didn't mute the obscenities coming out of her mouth as she stormed down the hallway to my room. Little did she know that I had already put away my books, straightened my long, choco-late-brown hair, and slipped on the little red dress she left hanging for me in my room while I was still asleep. I'd been right when I said I was going to sleep for twenty-four hours; once I got back from eating lunch with everyone, I passed out.

Before Gabriella could barge into my room, I quickly finished the last touches of my makeup and put it all away. I was ready to go.

The second Gabriella burst through my door and saw me, her eyes went wide and she stepped back, amazed. "Wow, you look so freaking hot right now."

Waltzing into my room, she whistled and took me in from head to toe, nodding in approval. She looked amazing as well with her sleek, raven-black hair hanging down past her shoulders and wearing a skin tight black dress that hugged her curves. All of the girls on campus were jealous of her. Hell, sometimes I was … but I loved her.

"You are seriously going to turn heads tonight, Ash. I know you'll have a good time. Besides, you need to let loose and have some fun. Exams are over for now, and there's nothing holding you back. Maybe you could let one of the fighters loosen you up a bit," she said, waggling her eyebrows. "I'm pretty sure with all of that pent up aggres-sion, they'll *almost* be able to keep up with you."

We'll see, I thought to myself.

"Besides," Gabriella added with a wink. "I told my friends that I was bringing you and that you were a hard one to crack. The guys need a little challenge in their lives. Believe me, they never get that."

Sneaking into my bathroom, Gabriella grabbed my makeup bag and opened it so she could touch up her face with what I had. She'd always liked my makeup better than hers. "I'm almost positive they'll be what you're looking for," she called out.

So far none of the guys on campus were up to par with what I wanted ... well, all but one. Unfortunately, he was taken. I guess you could say I had particular tastes. Most of the guys I dated were older, more experienced. The last guy happened to be someone who'd retired from making porn movies.

He hadn't told me until after a year of being together, but I was in love with him; he was a good guy. When he moved to Canada to be with his family, we knew it wouldn't work. Nobody knew I dated a porn star other than Gabriella, and she thought it was awesome.

Tonight we were going to the Staples Center in Los Angeles to watch her brother and her friends fight. I had been to a couple of the fights with her over the past two years, but never to any of the after parties. That wasn't by our choice, but her brother's. He made it very clear he didn't want her hanging out with his friends for fear of her getting hurt.

Believe me, we tried to soften him up, but nothing worked. He was an overprotective, stubborn ass male who couldn't see that his little sister had finally grown up and was in the real world. If he knew all of the stuff she'd done in her years in college he'd have a heart attack.

To be able to hang out with some of the sexiest, hard-core fighters in the UFC was going to be a night I wasn't going to forget. However, even if I did want to hook up with one of them I had a code to live by.

Yes, I was single and I could do anything I wanted, but I wasn't the type of girl to fall at anyone's feet and spread my legs, which was why I had no luck in finding a decent college boy. All they wanted was a quick fuck and that was it. I wanted the chase, the tension, the angst ... the passion.

When Gabriella was done touching up her makeup, she came back into my room and sprayed on some of my perfume. "What *friends* are you talking about exactly?" I asked. "You never told me who you picked up at the station."

Setting down my perfume, she smiled and started for the bedroom door. "I didn't, did I?"

I slipped on my red heels and grabbed my purse, following her out to the living room. "Nope. Spill it! And how do you know they can keep up with me? Being a fighter doesn't mean you're good in bed."

Gabriella shook her head and laughed, grabbing her keys off the kitchen table. "Trust me, Ash, they can keep up with you. I know what you like and I have no doubt they'll live up to your expectations." After exiting the apartment, she locked the door. "You know, it's kind of sad really, but I have to live vicariously through you since my brother would kill me if I got with one of his friends. I just want you to have fun."

"Oh, Gabriella, you could always have your fun with one of them and keep it a secret. I'm pretty sure they wouldn't be stupid enough to tell your brother."

Gabriella laughed. "True, but I don't know if anyone would risk it."

There *was* one fighter she talked about a lot, and even though she denied it, I knew it pissed her off that she couldn't pursue him. I felt bad for her.

"So again, Gabby, how do you know these guys can

keep up with me if you haven't ever slept with any of them?" I asked curiously, lifting my brows teasingly.

Looping her arm through mine, she pulled me down the stairs so we could be on our way. "Oh, now don't you dare go insinuating anything. I've heard stories from some of the groupies at the fights, and let me tell you, they're pretty crazy."

I was intrigued.

"Do tell then," I murmured excitedly. "Are we talking kinky kind of crazy, or just mind blowing sex crazy?"

When we got to the car, Gabriella faced me, grinning. "Oh, believe me, it's interesting all right, especially when I tell you that it's the *twins* I'm talking about."

Ah, yes, I should've known ... the Jameson twins. I could only imagine the kinds of things they were guilty of.

I'd seen them both of them fight, and on occasion Gabriella would go and hang out with them when I was busy studying. I'd never forget the times when Gabriella and I would go to Matt's room after the fights were over, and there would be a slew of women waiting outside of the twins' door to see if they'd catch their eyes. It was the most ridiculous thing I'd ever seen.

There was no way in hell I would stand there like a bitch in heat, begging for their attention; it was pathetic. Thank God, I wasn't like that. If I was, I'd probably kill myself just to put me out of my misery.

If there was anything I knew for certain, it was that I needed to stay away from those twins. Even though I hadn't ever officially met them, I could see it in their eyes when they fought... they were trouble. *Double trouble.*

There were plenty of other fighters I could take a chance with.

CHAPTER 7

Ashleigh

AS SOON AS we got to the arena, we walked past the mile long line at the front and went inside to find our front row seats. I guess it was the perks of having a friend with a superstar older brother. I never really thought I would like MMA fighting when I first started going with Gabriella, but they were actually kind of exciting. Hearing the crowd roar and cheer for their favorite fighters was intoxicating; I loved the energy.

"I'm telling you, this night is going to be amazing," Gabriella chimed, elbowing me in the side. "I've missed the carefree Ash I had a blast with over the summer. Now that fall break is here, we can let loose and have fun like we did at the beach."

"You mean with Bradley," I quipped. "You two are

going to drive me insane. Why don't you just go out with him already?"

She shrugged, but smiled as her gaze landed on something behind me. A guy wearing a fitted red T-shirt and jeans with short, jet-black hair and striking blue eyes headed in our direction with a smile on his face.

"Hey, Cole," Gabriella squealed while jumping in his arms. "Are you not fighting tonight?"

Chuckling, he held her for a moment before sitting her down. "I am, but I thought I would watch some of the other fights while I had time."

"Are you coming to the party tonight?"

"No, I'm going back to Vegas. Tyler will be there, though. I know he'll be happy to see you." He winked, making Gabriella blush. "Maybe next time I'll be able to party with you. Have fun and stay out of trouble. I'm sure you know what I'm talking about."

He tapped her on the chin, grinning at both of us, and strolled back to his seat. "What was that about?" I asked. "What did he mean by his last comment?"

Gabriella waved me off. "Oh, he just knows about my brother's warning for me to stay away from them."

I didn't believe her, not for one second.

"Okay, liar. If you don't want to tell me, that's fine. I have to say, though, I'm kind of jealous you know all of these bad ass UFC fighters. I wish I could trade places with you."

"No you don't," she groaned. "You know how my brother is and it's a pain in the ass. I can't get anywhere near the guys without someone watching me. I bet you a million dollars Matt has someone following me tonight."

"Are you interested in any of them?" I asked, knowing very well she was. She never told me his name, and always seemed to change the subject when I'd ask. However, by the way she blushed at the mention of Tyler, I had a feeling it was him.

Quickly, Gabriella shook her head. "No, I'm not interested in any of them. Besides, tonight isn't all about me, it's about you. We finished our exams and it's time to celebrate. I want you to put all thoughts of classes aside and have some fun. Promise me!"

She stared at me with those piercing green eyes and never once wavered. No matter what I did, I knew she wouldn't give up until I promised. Holding my hands up in defeat, I chuckled and said, "Okay, I promise. Although, I'm starting to think I'm going to regret this."

Gabriella smirked. "Oh, believe me, you'll enjoy every minute of it. I say we get wild and crazy tonight."

Get a few drinks in me and I'll be good to go.

"Done," I complied with a smile.

The lights flashed and the music blared as fighter after fighter entered the ring, round after round, and fought their way to the top. I cringed when one time I heard the audible snap of a guy getting his arm broken because he wouldn't tap out when the other had him in a ridiculously tight hold.

There was a ton of blood, sweat, and tears as each fighter pounded on the other. It was a brutal sport, but the excitement was exhilarating.

After watching the first set of fights, ranging from the Flyweight to Welterweight, it was soon time for the Middleweight, Light Heavyweight, and the Heavyweight fighters to go on. The announcer entered the ring with his crisp black tux and slicked back gray hair, holding the microphone up to his lips.

He waved at the crowd, and his enigmatic voice boomed through the speakers, "Ladies and gentlemen, the time has come for our Middleweight division. I'm sure you all know what that means, right?"

The crowd exploded in cheers, as did Gabriella, who almost burst my left ear drum with her screams. Grin spreading wider, the announcer nodded his head and chuckled. "That's right, everyone. The Twins of Terror have entered the building and they're coming to wreak havoc. Fighting first tonight is RYLEY 'THE RAM-PAGE' JAAMMMEEESSOONNNN! Come on out!"

I covered my ears and hoped the ringing would stop as the ladies behind me screamed louder than the whole arena put together. *Great, I'll probably go deaf by the time I'm thirty.* The lights dimmed for a second, but suddenly the room exploded in swiveling multi-colored lights and the song "The Pride" by Five Finger Death Punch, blaring over the speakers.

Ryley came out with his head down, covered in a royal blue robe, which was open to reveal his white and blue shorts and a set of perfectly conditioned, glistening abs. One lady jumped over the railing and flung herself into his arms, attempting to kiss him, but was quickly hauled off by the security guards.

"Wow, these women are crazy," I said to Gabriella.

"Yeah, tell me about it. Matt's told me all about the kinds of women he messed around with after his fights."

I could only imagine.

When Ryley got up into the ring and took off his robe, he circled around and lifted his hands up arrogantly in the air while the crowd cheered. From his right shoulder, all the way down his arm, were tattoos, along with another one across the top of his back. I loved tattooed men.

Gabriella hollered his name. Almost immediately, he found her in the crowd and smiled; although, not before raking his gaze toward me with a mischievous tilt to his lips.

Nudging me in the side, Gabriella playfully warned, "Uh-oh, Ash, he's noticed you. I've seen that look on him before."

Biting my lip, I lifted a curious brow, never taking my gaze away from him. "And what exactly does that mean?"

Gabriella put her hand around my arm and squeezed. "It means, my dear friend, that he has his eyes on you. He'll find you at the party tonight, I'm sure of it."

"Yeah, well, I don't know what he hopes to gain by that."

Gabriella scoffed, "Yes, you do, Ash. You look hot tonight, and any guy in this room, and specifically at the party, will notice you. He's going to have some competition."

"Good," I chuckled. "I don't want it to be easy for him like I'm sure it is with every other girl he chases."

While Ryley waited for his opponent to get into the ring, he kept sneaking glances my way, winking at me every time I would meet his gaze. *Arrogant bastard.* His dark blond hair was gelled into messy spikes, and even though I didn't want them to … his eyes were what captured me. Even from down in my seat I could tell they were the most beautiful blue I'd ever seen; almost hypnotizing.

Whatever you do, don't look at his eyes, I hissed at

myself, turning my head. They were dangerous.

As soon as the fight began, I couldn't help but look up at him, at the way his body moved gracefully across the mat. His punches were hard and precise, but what got me more was that he knew he was a god in the ring. I could see it in the arrogant smirk he kept permanently splayed on his face, and by the way he laughed when his opponent would overthrow a punch. He absolutely dominated every single move.

I wonder if he's like that in the bedroom.

Once down on the mat, his opponent in a vice-like grip, Ryley peered over at me as if he'd heard what I was thinking. His heated gaze made my clit throb, and when I crossed my legs tight, he gave me a knowing smirk. Rolling my eyes, I crossed my arms over my chest and looked at anything and everything other than him.

"Are you okay?" Gabriella asked with a glint sparkling in her eye.

Quickly, I waved her off. "Yes, I'm fine. I think I just need a drink. Do you want one?" *Or maybe even a cold shower.*

Really, I just wanted to get away from the ring and Ryley's hypnotic blue gaze. Gabriella shook her head, returning her focus to the fight. "No, I'm good. Thank you, though. Just make sure you hurry back."

Getting up from my seat, I didn't even look at Ryley in the ring before rushing out of the arena. I breathed a sigh of relief as soon as I was away from the crowd … away from the thunderous cheers that I assumed meant Ryley had finally won. It didn't surprise me because the other guy hadn't stood a chance. I had to give it to Ryley, he was a good fighter.

At one of the concession stands, I waited in line and ordered a bottle of water even though I wasn't really thirsty. Still, I opened it up and took sips of it as I walked around. There weren't many people since another fight had just started, so I took my time and strolled around, glancing at all of the different merchandising carts.

There were T-shirts with the different fighters, and of course, there were ones with the Twins of Terror on them. It was uncanny how Ryley and Camden looked so much alike.

Fifteen minutes later my phone buzzed in my purse and I cringed. *Shit, Gabriella was going to kill me for being away for so long.* However, when I looked down at my phone it was a text from an unavailable number.

Hey, it's Gabriella. Turn to your right and go all the way down the hall until you get to the guard. He'll let you by. It's the second door on the left. Just walk on in.

Wait, what? Why wasn't she still watching the fights?

Feeling a little strange, I did as the text said and walked all the way down to where the guard was stationed by another large door. Beyond that was where the fighters had their separate rooms so that they could get dressed and warm up before the fights.

The guard nodded as I approached and stepped out of the way, allowing me to pass, and when I did it was like I was in another world. Some of the fighters whistled and made suggestive comments as I stood there, looking down at the text one more time.

It said to go to the second door on the left and just walk in. I prayed it wasn't Gabriella's brother, trying to persuade her not to go to the party tonight after he'd already said she could.

Ready to defend her if need be, I held my head high and opened the door … only to have my heart thunder out of my chest at what was in front of me; it sure as hell wasn't Gabriella's brother.

There sat Ryley with a smug smile on his face, all bare-chested and glistening in sweat, a white towel wrapped around his shoulders and a bottle of water in his hands. He raked his clear blue eyes up and down my body and I froze, hating that he had that affect on me.

"What the hell?" I snapped. "Where's Gabriella?"

Picking up his phone, he waved it in the air and sat it back down. "Oh, she's not here. She's getting ready to watch her brother fight, but she *did* give me your number when I asked her for it. Surely you don't mind, right?"

I crossed my arms at the chest and glared at him. "Actually, I do mind. I don't do well with tricks, *Mr. Jameson.* If you wanted to talk to me you should've approached me like a normal person instead of being all stalkerish. It's kind of creepy."

In a way, it was actually kind of hot, but I wasn't going to tell him that.

Taken aback, Ryley opened his mouth to speak and then shut it, only to open it again. "Wow, I must say I haven't had anyone ever say that to me. Most women like my tactics." Slowly, he got up from the couch and stalked toward me, his gaze curious and heated.

"What do you want?" I asked, taking a step away.

He set his bottle of water down on the small table beside the couch, along with the towel wrapped around his neck, before turning his blue gaze in my direction. "I wanted to see if you would be my date tonight for the party. I figured I would snag you up before Gabriella showed you off to everyone. I don't want someone else getting to you first."

"Really? That's what you called me in here for?" I asked incredulously. He started to take a step forward and I instantly moved back, swallowing hard. "Sorry, but I'm taken."

When my back hit the wall, I gritted my teeth and took short, shallow breaths as he continued to move closer. My heart pounded relentlessly, especially when he hovered over me and leaned down toward my ear, breathing me in. His bare skin grazed against my chest, making me shiver, and even more so when he moaned in approval, his warm breath tickling my ear. My eyes fluttered shut and I bit my lip to keep myself from moaning in return.

"I don't like it when people are dishonest with me, Ashleigh. Gabriella already told me you were single and I know she wouldn't lie to me."

My eyes snapped open. *I am so going to kill her.*

"You don't even know me," I challenged. "Why do you want me to be your date? You saw me for one second when you were up in the ring. I could be the biggest bitch in the world for all you know."

"That could be true. If you want the honest truth," he said, gazing down my body, "I saw you in that red dress and all I could think about was how hot it would be to fuck you in it."

Holding in my gasp, I tightened my legs together to keep my clit from throbbing out of control. It pissed me off that my body responded to him, but it could also be because he was so close; brushing his heated body against mine, and smelling so amazingly delicious. The wild side of me wanted to tell him to take me right then and there, but the logical side wanted to slap the shit out of him.

"Do you honestly get women by saying stuff like that?" I asked dryly, without a hint of a smile.

His grin grew wider. "Most of the time. So what do you say? Do you want to be my date for the night ... the *whole* night?"

Yes, my mind screamed at me.

"No," I snapped, making his smug smile disappear. "I'm not one of your little groupies, Ryley, and I sure as hell am not going to beg for your attention like what you're used to. You need to find someone else. I'm not interested."

You just lied again, I scolded myself.

Turning on my heel, I headed for the door and opened it, only to be stopped by a hand grasping my arm and the door shutting quickly in front of me. "Don't you see? I don't want anyone else. I saw *you* and *you* are what I want."

Laughing, I turned around and yanked my arm out of his hold. "Tell that to someone who'll believe you, Ryley. I don't fall that easily, especially for someone who hasn't had to work for a woman. You'll have to do much better than that."

Or else I'm not going to play the game.

CHAPTER

8

Ashleigh

BY THE TIME I got back to Gabriella, the fights were over and she was talking to her brother. He had the same dark hair and green eyes as her; however, he was huge, nothing but pure muscle with tattoos all over his body. Definitely an extremely good looking guy, but he was taken by one of the most reputable journalists in all of the country. She was definitely a lucky woman.

"Hey, Ashleigh, what's up?" he asked as I approached.

While I stood there seething, Gabriella had the gall to look innocent. "Oh, nothing much really, just had a run in with Ryley. It appears your sister has a knack for playing tricks."

Matt sighed and shook his head, pinning a lethal glare

at his sister. "Gabby, you know better than to set her up with him. All he wants is a good time and that's it."

"Well, what makes you think that Ashleigh doesn't want the same thing?" she countered defiantly, her hands on her hips. "Women can use men just as easily as men use them. Besides, the twins need to learn a lesson about humility and Ashleigh is the best candidate. I have full confidence that she'll put them in their place, or at least one of them."

I wasn't as confident as her, especially after my encounter with Ryley. There was something about him that made me nervous; I didn't know if I could tame him. His brother was more than likely the same way, although I had to admit, it *would* be kind of fun to try taming one of the Twins of Terror.

"Well," Matt started, looking over at me, "I agree the twins need to be taken down a notch or two. If you think you can do it, then by all means go for it. However, be forewarned, they've been known to break a few hearts."

"My heart doesn't break so easily," I told him honestly. "Besides, I turned him down."

Shaking her head, Gabriella snorted and put her arm around me. "I don't know how to tell you this, Ash, but I think you just made one of the biggest mistakes ever. He's not going to give up on you until he gets what he wants. He doesn't like to lose."

Rubbing my hands together, I smiled and bit my lip. "Well then, let the games begin."

The party for the night happened to be at none other than Ryley and Camden's house ... or at least at one of their homes. They had a couple of them on the California coast, and it just so happened they had one in the Los Angeles area. *Must be nice to have a shit ton of money.*

My family earned a decent amount, but they were very conservative with it. I honestly didn't see the point in having six different houses or a garage full of cars; it was a waste of money.

"I wouldn't go wandering off if I were you," Gabriella teased. "Otherwise, I might not see you until morning."

We got out of her little silver sports car and headed up to the door. There were so many people around it was crazy. "You have nothing to worry about. I don't plan on falling victim to Ryley's charms tonight."

Snickering, Gabriella opened the front door and ushered me inside. "That may be true, but I'm curious to know what you would say if both of the twins tried to get you tonight. They do have a habit of sharing things, you know. I'll admit, if I knew my brother wouldn't kill them I'd probably let them do whatever they wanted with me for the night."

"Really? You think they would be that good?" I asked skeptically.

Gabriella scoffed, "Please, from all of the stories I've heard, how could they not be."

I needed to hear those stories. I'd been with only a

handful of men, but never two at once. I honestly think I would go insane with just one of them … much less both. I had yet to meet Camden, but if he had the same pair of hypnotic blue eyes as his brother I'd probably give in without a second thought. *It may be best I don't meet him.*

Inside of the house, the lights were dimmed while everyone stood around talking, drinking, and dancing as the music blared from all around. As soon as I had some drinks in me, I planned on getting out there and having fun as well.

Over the loud music, Gabriella squealed and pulled on my arm, squeezing us through the crowd. "Oh my God, Ash, he's here!"

"Who?" I shouted, laughing as she pulled me along.

"It's Tyler, my brother's friend."

By the time we got across the room, my toes throbbed from being trampled on by the drunken dancers, but I sucked it up and kept walking. The last thing I wanted was to look like an idiot hobbling across the floor.

"Tyler!"

After she shouted out his name, she ran right up to him and he scooped her up into his arms. There was an awkward exchange where they almost looked like they wanted to kiss, but he set her down instead. *Interesting.* Gabriella ran her hands through his platinum blond hair and pursed her lips. "Now why did you cut your hair? It's all gone!"

Tyler shrugged. "I don't know. I guess I needed a change. I kind of like it short. Don't you?"

Gabriella sighed, and then smiled. "Of course I do. You're still the same Tyler even with shorter hair." Pulling me to her side, she waved back and forth between us. "I want you to meet my friend, Ashleigh. Ashleigh, this is my friend Tyler. Now you two talk while I get us some drinks."

Quickly, she scampered off and left us alone, but Tyler filled the awkwardness by extending his hand. "Hey, Ashleigh, it's nice to meet you. Do you go to school with Gabriella?"

Taking his hand, we both shook firmly and then let go. His eyes were a stormy gray, completely different from any color I'd ever seen; they were mesmerizing.

"I do," I replied. "I met her in one of our classes a couple of years ago. College life has definitely gotten a lot more exciting with her in it."

Tyler smiled and finished off his cup of beer. "I don't doubt that. She's definitely an interesting female."

"That she is," I mumbled.

About that time, Gabriella came back carrying two cups filled with some kind of red liquid. "Hey, I'm sorry it took so long. I kind of got sidetracked." Narrowing my eyes, she bit her lip and quickly nodded toward another fighter who I knew to be Paxton Emerson.

He was pretty hot with his dark hair, sea green eyes, and tattoos down his tanned arms, but he wasn't exactly one of the good guys. I didn't know many of the fighters, but his reputation was widely known; he was bad news.

Gabriella shook her head, clearly not wanting me to say anything. *I wonder what happened.* "The guy at the bar said it was a hurricane. I have no clue what that means or what's in it, but it looks good. Anyway," she said, holding out one of the cups for me, "bottoms up, baby."

Taking the cup, we both gulped ours down and almost immediately I could feel the warmth of the liquor seeping its way into my blood. Two drinks were definitely going to be my limit if they were that potent. The last thing I needed was to get drunk around a bunch of people I didn't know, especially Ryley and his brother.

Setting her cup on the mantle, Gabriella grabbed Tyler around the waist and shouted, "All right, you guys, it's time to get out there and dance. Let's go!"

"Oh hell, I'm in trouble now," Tyler teased, putting his arm across my shoulders and hers.

Pushing through the throng of people, we stopped in the middle of the floor; Tyler against my front with his hands around my waist, and Gabriella to his back. Some kind of techno song played over the surround sound, so I went with it and started to dance. If there was one thing I was good at, it was dancing.

Rolling my hips against Tyler's, I linked my hands around his neck as he held me firmly by my hips. I could feel a set of eyes watching me, and when I looked up at the top of the stairs, Ryley was there leaning over the banister, with his hardened gaze fastened on me. Smiling, I winked at him and waved before he stormed off.

Once the song was over, Gabriella and I switched places, which put me grinding against Tyler's ass while Gabriella took his front. I had to admit, Tyler had a very sexy backside.

Another thing I noticed and felt was the tension between him and Gabriella. I knew right then and there that they wanted each other. It was a shame they couldn't do anything about it because of her brother, especially since he and Tyler were best friends.

Smiling, I waved at Gabriella over Tyler's shoulder and left the dance area so I could get something to drink other than alcohol. The kitchen was just off to the right, through a set of double doors, and there were people everywhere milling about and talking. Thankfully, there were chilled bottles of water lined up on the bar.

I grabbed one and started to walk off ... but I didn't get very far. I heard Ryley and Camden's names being whispered among a group of women at a table in the corner, so needless to say, I sidled in closer to eavesdrop on what they were saying.

"Who do you think they'll pick tonight? They always try to find someone new to play with on fight nights," one of them whispered. She had way too much makeup on, and wore a dress that was so short her ass cheeks began to show as she leaned over to talk to the other women; she had beautiful sleek blonde hair, though.

So the twins wanted someone to play with, huh?

There was another girl with curly, red hair wearing a green tank top and denim shorts that spoke up next. Her voice was quieter, so I moved closer to listen. "Well, you know what happened to April, don't you? Ryley let her go because he didn't like the way she sucked his dick. Yeah, she left all pissed off. Talk about crazy, right? I wish they would give me a chance. I would love to see if I could handle them both at the same time."

"Excuse me," I said, cutting in. "I'm sorry to barge in on your conversation, but I couldn't help overhearing. Are you saying that Ryley and Camden look for women that'll sleep with them both ... at the same time?"

The girl with the red hair nodded her head. "Yes, it's like a game to them. Every Saturday night at these parties they both find a girl they're interested in and proposition her. My friend April was picked last week, but she was let go."

There were five of them huddled together and I couldn't help but wonder …

"So, is that the reason why you are all here tonight? Hoping you get picked?" I asked curiously. It had to be the saddest thing I'd ever heard.

"Of course that's why we're here," the red-haired girl replied incredulously.

Taking my bottle of water, I backed up slowly and smiled, even though I really wanted to tell them how stupid they were. "Well, all right then. You ladies have a wonderful night and I wish you luck."

Turning around quickly, I waltzed out of the room and past the gigantic living room where Gabriella and Tyler were still dancing. There weren't as many people outside, so I decided to go out there and sit by the pool to get some fresh air.

Now that the sun was gone, it was chilly—especially when the brisk wind blew across my bare skin—causing steam to billow up from the pool. Once I sat down on the edge and lowered my feet inside its warm depths, I sighed and leaned back on my hands, gazing up at the clear night sky.

It was quiet and I loved it, at least until …

"We could go for a swim if you'd like," a voice called out behind me.

Groaning, I turned my head and watched Ryley walk down the steps toward me. He was dressed in a pair of ripped denim jeans and a white T-shirt with a navy baseball cap covering up his blond hair. However, there was something different about him in the way he carried himself and in the way he spoke; his tattoos were also on the wrong arm. Then it dawned on me ... it wasn't Ryley. It was his brother, Camden.

"Let me guess, your brother told you to come out here and talk to me?" I asked dryly.

Narrowing his gaze, he held out his hand and I let him help me up. He was about six foot tall, but once I slipped on my red heels I was only shy of that by maybe an inch. "Actually, I haven't spoken to my brother," he responded truthfully. "I take it that you have, though. What did he say to you?"

Keeping his hold on my hand, he led me back up the steps toward the house, but stopped in front of the doors. "He wanted me to be his date tonight," I told him. "I assumed you both talked it out before approaching your prospective conquests."

Camden lowered his head and chuckled, but when he looked up I almost faltered. He had the same damn hypnotic blue eyes and smile as Ryley. Holy hell, they were going to kill me.

"I take it you've already heard, huh?"

"Yeah, it's kind of hard not to considering you have a house full of women salivating at the chance to have sex with you two. They told me about the little game you and your brother like to play," I replied snarkily.

Camden moved closer and tilted my chin up with his warm fingers. "You don't sound like you're down for a little fun. It's sad, really. After watching you tonight, you're the only one here that I think would be able to handle us ... and enjoy it."

Taking a deep breath, I let it out slowly and lifted my lips to his, but stopped once I could feel the heat of his breath brushing across them. He wrapped his arms around my waist and pulled me in tighter, his hard cock pressing against my stomach. I had to hand it to him and his brother; they didn't waste any time.

"I'm going to tell you what I told your brother," I whispered, sliding my thigh in between his legs, torturing him.

Groaning, he lowered his hands to my ass and squeezed. "Please tell me you said you'd be ours tonight. If he wants you as bad as I do then it'll be a night you won't forget."

Grabbing his wrists, I pried his hands away from my ass and took a step away. "And that right there is one of the reasons why I told him no," I admitted forcefully.

Camden lowered his arms and furrowed his brows. "So are you trying to say that's not something you'd want? That makes no sense."

"I didn't say it's not something I'd want, but you see, you make it sound like it's a privilege to have sex with you. Haven't you ever thought about how it might be the opposite way around? What if *you* were the ones lucky enough to have the one woman for the night? I'm not a one night stand kind of girl, and believe me, if I was you wouldn't know what the hell to do with me."

Eyes wide, his mouth dropped open, and on that last note, I opened the glass door and marched inside. The five girls that I talked to in the kitchen had all seen the interaction between me and Camden, and of course, I was met with lethal stares as I walked past.

"Don't worry, ladies, he's still up for grabs," I said in passing as I headed toward the front door.

Gabriella caught up to me and laughed. "Oh my God, Ash, you should've seen his face when you walked off.

Everyone was watching you two, and even Ryley was speechless when he saw you walk away. I don't think I've ever seen that before."

"Yeah, well, I can't say that walking away was the best option. Now I'm going to wonder for the rest of my life what it would've been like to be with them. I'll admit, I wanted to give in."

Wrapping her arm around my waist, Gabriella walked me out the front door and down to her car. "I think you might be the only female in existence that's turned them down, Ash. It was a smart move, though, and I have to say that you definitely put them in their place tonight."

I laughed and squeezed her tight. "You're damn right I did, and it felt so freaking good, too."

Now I wonder what desperate female they'll pick tonight since I turned them down.

Once we got to the car and backed out of the driveway, I took one last look at Ryley and Camden's home, wishing deep down that I could've gotten a small sample of what it would've been like to be with them. *I guess I'll never know, but I can always fantasize.* Hopefully, we had a pack of batteries at the apartment ... because I was going to need them.

CHAPTER 9

Ashleigh

THE WEEKEND WAS over and it was time to get my mind back into books and school. That was easier said than done considering I'd been reading the same page over and over. *Stop thinking about them, Ash.*

No more daydreaming about the dimples in their cheeks when they smiled, the way they smelled, or the way their blue eyes heated up every time they saw you. *Oh whatever, Ashleigh*, I scolded myself. It was probably the way they looked at every girl just to draw them in.

I didn't even realize that class was over until Gabriella shook me by the shoulders and hollered in my ear, making me jump. "Wake up, girl! Class is over."

The room was empty.

"You got it bad, you know that? Maybe you

should've let the Twins of Terror rock your world this weekend," she teased.

Rolling my eyes, I packed up my books and followed her out of the room. "Yeah, well, it's too late now."

"I'm sure if you called them they'd be up for it," she chuckled.

Shaking my head, I snorted. "Screw that."

It was lunch time, so we walked outside to our favorite spot on campus underneath the giant black oak tree where Colin and Bradley sat waiting on us. Both guys were perfectly tanned and shirtless, which didn't make it easy to concentrate around them.

Every single girl that walked by couldn't help but stare at them and give us evil looks in the process. The guys enjoyed the attention, especially Bradley who loved it even more when the girls would look at him when Gabriella was around. Unfortunately, she never seemed to care.

Bradley had caramel-colored hair and the eyes to match with the cutest set of dimples in his cheeks. I didn't let those dimples fool me, though; he may look innocent, but he wasn't.

I sat down next to Colin while Gabriella sat beside Bradley, trying her best to hide her smile. "Are you okay, Ash?" Colin asked, stealing one of my chips after I pulled them out. "You look like something's wrong."

"Nope, I'm fine."

In my bag, I fetched the ham sandwich I'd made earlier this morning and broke it in half, eating only a couple bites of it. "Did something happen at the party?" he asked, his jaw clenched tight, waiting on my answer.

Sighing, I handed him the rest of my chips and the last half of my ham sandwich; food was the last thing on my mind.

"Oh, she's fine," Gabriella cut in with a smirk on her face. "She's just a little … um … frustrated. She hung out with some of my friends this weekend, and it was very interesting might I say. Why don't you give them the story, Ash?"

Groaning, I leaned my head against the tree and looked up at the crisp, green leaves gracing the branches. "Trust me, they don't want to hear the story. There's nothing to tell anyway."

Colin tensed beside of me. "Ash, what did you do? You didn't—"

"No," I blurted out, glancing over at him. "I didn't do what you think I did."

"Nope, she didn't," Gabriella chimed. "In fact, she blew them off and it was so freaking funny. She made history last night."

I rolled my eyes and laughed while throwing a potato chip at her. "I wouldn't exactly call it that, but it *was* kind of epic."

Colin smiled, but before I could return the gesture, something over his shoulder caught my attention. "Holy shit," I growled, reaching for his baseball cap.

His eyes went wide and he turned his head to peer behind him. "What is it?"

Slipping his hat over my head, I pulled my ponytail through the back and grabbed one of my textbooks so I could hold it in front of my face. Ryley and Camden were on the opposite side of the quad, walking around the campus.

I had no idea know how I spotted them so quickly with such a large crowd, but it was them … they were there. What the hell were they doing on campus?

One of them was in a pair of navy Adidas gym shorts and a white tank top; the other was in a pair of jeans, red T-shirt, and navy blue baseball cap. Camden wore that same hat the other night, but there was no way I could tell them apart being so far away.

I did know that Ryley was the one with the jagged scar at his hairline and that they both smelled completely different. However, I wasn't planning on getting that close to tell them apart.

"Gabriella, don't you dare turn around. I don't want them to see me," I snapped, peering at her over the top of my book before glaring at the twins.

She froze in place, but Bradley and Colin glanced in the direction of my glare. "Surely you're not talking about the douche bag look-alike motherfuckers, right?" Bradley asked incredulously.

Gasping, Gabriella put a hand over her mouth and quickly turned her head. "Oh my God, they're here?" She swiveled back around and smacked Bradley in the arm. "And don't talk about them like that. They're my friends, and professional UFC fighters. I definitely wouldn't call them douche bag look-alike motherfuckers to their faces."

Bradley scoffed, "I'm not worried about that, sweetheart. I can hold my own."

And he probably could, but that was the last thing we needed.

"Why would they be looking for you?" Colin asked. "Didn't you say you turned them down?"

I groaned and hid behind my book. "Yeah, I did."

He sighed and tilted the book away from my face. "Are you sure about that?"

"She did, Colin," Gabriella chimed, smirking at me. "Although, I did tell her that since she turned them down they'd only try harder to get her. They're not the type to give up."

Colin moved closer to me, his arms touching mine. "Do you need me to help you get rid of them?"

"I'll help, too," Bradley stated excitedly.

Eyes wide, I quickly shook my head. "No, don't do that. They're probably not looking for me anyway."

Yeah, right. You know they are.

Ryley and Camden hadn't seen me yet and I hoped that they wouldn't. I had no makeup on, and was dressed in a pair of denim shorts, a green tank top, and a pair of brown Rainbow sandals. I didn't exactly look glamorous at the moment.

"Uh … I think they are because they're headed straight this way, Ash," Colin whispered, putting his arm around my shoulders. "I don't think they've seen you, but they recognized Gabriella. Just play along with me, okay?"

"Okay," I whispered back, keeping the book in front of my face.

"Hey guys," Gabriella squealed. "What brings you over here? I figured you would be training right now."

"We were," one of them said, "but we wanted to find Ashleigh and we figured she'd be with you. Do you know where she is?"

Please don't tell them, I repeated over and over in my mind. My palms began to sweat, but I kept hold of the book in front of my face.

Thankfully, Gabriella didn't hesitate. "Um … no, actually I don't. We had a class together this morning, but that's the only time I'll see her until the afternoon at the apartment."

Their voices were so much alike I couldn't tell which one was speaking. "All right, well tell her we were looking for her. We need to talk to her about something."

"Oh-kay," Gabriella drawled out slowly. "I can't guarantee you that she'll call you, but I'll tell her you were looking for her."

"Thanks, Gabby. Tell your brother we said hey. We hate that he couldn't come to the party the other night."

"Will do, guys. I'm sure I'll see you in a couple of weeks."

"You better," one of them called out, their voice sounding further away.

"Are they leaving?" I whispered to Colin.

He nodded, but kept his gaze forward. A few seconds later, he lowered the book and both Gabriella and Bradley smirked at me. "You're safe," she giggled. "They didn't suspect a thing."

Colin slid his arm away from my shoulders and turned to look at me, his gaze concerned. "What exactly do they want with you?"

That was a good question. I wanted to know the same thing.

While quickly packing up my books, I sent a warning glare to Gabriella so she'd know I didn't want them knowing anything about what happened over the weekend. "Nothing you would want to know, trust me. All right, guys, I'm out of here. I need to head to the library before my next class."

"Do you want me to go with you?" Gabriella asked hesitantly. "I can walk you there before I leave to go back home."

Getting to my feet, I took off Colin's hat and gave it back to him, sighing. "No, Gabby, I'll be fine. I'll see you at home in just a bit." I hurried off and waved them good-bye as I headed toward the library.

What the hell have I gotten myself into?

I was curious to know what they wanted, but I knew it would only mean trouble if I did. The decision was simple enough … I wasn't going to call. If they wanted to talk to me bad enough they would try to find me again.

And it just so happened that they did.

"Well, hello there, sexy," a voice spoke out right behind me, making me gasp. Stopping mid-stride, I closed my eyes and held my breath, hoping it was just my imagination playing tricks on me.

When I opened them up, my fears became reality; both Ryley and Camden stood before me with smug expressions on their faces. I was right before when I thought Ryley was the one in the shorts and tank top because right above his left eye at the hairline was the small jagged scar. Camden was the one in the jeans, T-shirt, and baseball cap. It was uncanny how much they looked alike.

"You didn't think you were fooling us back there, did you?" Camden asked.

His striking blue eyes were almost hidden below his hat, but it definitely didn't hide the mischievous leer or the way he bit his lip. I glared at them both before walking right past them with my head held high. Unfortunately, that didn't stop them; they both fell into step beside me, one on each side.

"I wasn't trying to fool you at all. I figured you would've been smart enough to realize that I had no interest in talking to you."

They both chuckled, but it was Ryley who spoke next. "When are you going to stop lying, Ashleigh? I already told you I don't like it when people lie. I know you're just as interested in us as we are with you."

Keep walking, Ashleigh. Keep your head straight and don't stop.

"Oh yeah, and how do you know that?" I snapped, picking up my pace.

Abruptly grabbing my hand, Ryley pulled me over to a secluded corner and blocked me in against the brick wall of the library. Other students walked by, but none of them seemed to see us in the darkened corner.

"What are you doing?" I hissed. They both stood in front of me with a hand against the wall, caging me in.

"We just want to talk. Do you want to know how I know you're lying?" Ryley asked, moving his body closer.

He nuzzled my neck with his nose and breathed me in before placing a gentle kiss behind my ear. "I can see it in your eyes, angel. You may be able to lie with those luscious lips of yours, but your eyes tell me everything. I understand you're pissed right now, but it's not because we have you cornered, it's because you want us and you're fighting against it. What is it that you don't want? Is it because you want something more and you know that's not what we can give you?"

"No," I huffed. "I'm not stupid enough to believe either of you could ever love someone enough to be faithful. Believe me, I'm in college and the last thing I want is something serious."

"Then what is it?" Camden asked, leaning into my other side. With Ryley on my right and Camden on my left, I thought I'd go insane. They each had a hand on my waist, and both leaned in to kiss along the sides of my neck, gently grazing their teeth along my skin.

"I don't want you to give me anything," I whispered breathlessly. "I'm worth more than being just another mark on your belt that you forget. I bet you've already forgotten about the girl you fucked after I left the other night."

They both paused and pulled back. "There wasn't anyone after you left," Camden growled. "I think we made it perfectly clear that we wanted *you*. Just hear us out, and if you don't like our proposition we'll leave you alone."

Ryley smiled and twirled the hair of my ponytail in between his fingers. "Come on, angel, you know you have to be somewhat curious."

I groaned, glaring at them both. "I already know what your proposition is. You like to share your women, and if they don't meet your standards you let them go. I'm sorry, boys, but I'm not up for that. I have better things to do than get played with."

Glancing down at my phone, I realized I only had two minutes to get to my next class before they locked the doors. "Okay, this has been fun, but I have to go. Besides, this isn't exactly the place to talk about a threesome or whatever the hell it is you want with me."

Both guys glanced at each other quickly and nodded before turning back to me. "Then meet us tonight," Ryley suggested heatedly. "We want to do something different with you, but first we need to know the truth. If you say no, we'll leave here and never bother you again."

"What truth?" I asked.

He leaned down to my ear, and his warm breath tickled its way all the down my body to the very core between my legs. "Do you want us, Ashleigh? And don't lie to me because I'll be able to tell. We want to know if there's any part of you that craves our touch like we do yours. All we want is the truth."

My heart pounded in my chest; it was so loud I was sure they could both hear it. There was no denying that I wanted them, just to know what it would be like to experience the pleasure of two men ... and best of all, twins.

Was I really going to go through with this? I asked myself.

Yes, I most certainly was.

"Fine," I murmured huskily. "I want you both. Now what do we do."

"Right now you go to class," Camden stated.

"And tonight we'll come pick you up so we can discuss everything. Be ready by seven, angel," Ryley added.

They both kissed me on the cheek and left me in the corner. "Oh my God," I whispered quietly to myself; my eyes wide and my heart pumping wildly in my chest. "This is absolute craziness."

CHAPTER 10

Ashleigh

IT WAS HALF past six when Gabriella knocked on my door and stuck her head in. "Are you sure you want to do this?" she asked, opening the door wide. "They'll be here in thirty minutes."

Glancing at myself in the mirror, I applied the last touches of my makeup and ran my fingers through my wavy, brown hair. Dressing sexy wasn't on the agenda for the night, so I'd decided to wear a pair of jeans and a little yellow tank top.

"I'm as ready as I'll ever be, Gabby. We're only talking tonight, so nothing is going to happen," I replied, sighing.

Gabriella nodded and came in to sit on my bed. "All I can say is good luck. I think I'm kind of envious of you right now. It sucks because none of my brother's friends ever ask me out. They're afraid of pissing him off."

"There's always Bradley," I suggested slyly. "He is so into you it's ridiculous. Surely, you have to know that. Maybe you should give him a call and hang out tonight."

She shrugged before jumping off the bed. "Yeah, I guess I will. Good luck, and whatever you do, don't get attached to the twins. I don't want to see you get wrapped up in them and get your heart broken."

That was the last thing I was going to let happen.

"Don't worry about me, babe. I know how to keep my heart out of it. Besides, these boys need to be taught a lesson."

When the doorbell rang, Gabriella immediately ran out of my room, her footsteps thundering down the hallway. Taking a deep breath, I let it out slowly and waited a few seconds before waltzing out of my bedroom.

I could hear one of the twins talking, and when I turned the corner to the living room, I saw Camden. He had on his baseball cap, and was wearing the same red T-shirt and jeans from earlier today.

His gaze quickly found mine and he smiled. "Hey, are you ready to go?" he asked.

Nodding, I grabbed my purse and walked toward the door. "Where's Ryley?"

He followed behind me and placed his hand on the small of my back, making me shiver; unfortunately, he noticed it and smirked mischievously at me. "He's at the house getting everything ready for us. Are you hungry?"

"Kind of," I said, opening the door.

"Good, because you're eating dinner with us. We figured it would soften you up a bit."

"Do you always cook your prospective one night stands dinner?" I inquired curiously.

Chuckling, Camden reached for my hand so that he could hold it while we walked down the stairs. "Actually, no. Usually, we get straight to the point, but like we said earlier … things have changed this time. We have a new proposition for you that we've never offered anyone else."

I'm intrigued. One point for the Jameson twins.

He led me to his car—a metallic silver Mercedes SLS Roadster—which didn't surprise me at all. The twins liked to stand out, and in that car they definitely would. It was worth a whole hell of a lot more than my Toyota Camry.

Not expecting Camden to open the door for me, I was shocked when he kept hold of my hand and lifted the handle, ushering me inside. I slid in slowly, shivering as the cold leather chilled the skin on my back.

Very nice.

As soon as we got onto the road, Camden reached for my hand and turned it over, tracing small circles into my palm and along my wrist. "So why do you and your brother like to share women?" I asked curiously. "I would think two men like you would be a little more territorial."

His gaze darkened for a moment, but then he chuckled, deep and almost sinister. "We like to share when we don't give a fuck. It's fun to be able to be with a woman and fulfill her fantasies of having two lovers at the same time. You see, when a woman is taken to that level of pleasure, there's nothing she wouldn't do since she's in that state of mind. Ryley and I get what we want and so does she. It's a win-win situation. However, with you we both want you to ourselves. That's why we came up with our new plan."

"So basically what you're saying is that I'm *not* going to be with you both at the same time? What if that's what I wanted?"

The thought was tempting, but I honestly didn't know if I could go through with it. I guess there could be a first time for everything, right?

"I didn't say that," Camden replied with a smile. "After everything is said and done, the choice will be yours."

The choice will be mine? Oh hell.

When we arrived at the house, Camden put his arm around my waist and led me inside. It was much different considering the last time I was there it was loud and overrun with hundreds of people. Now it was quiet, the smell of Italian spices wafting from the kitchen.

"Honey, we're home," Camden called out jokingly.

On the kitchen table were three place settings, all with a plate of lasagna, bowl of salad, and a glass of white wine. It smelled like heaven, and my mouth began to water … only it wasn't just the food causing it.

Dressed in a pair of ripped denim jeans and not wearing a shirt, Ryley smiled at me. He hungrily gazed up and down my body, and I couldn't help but return the gesture, watching his tatted muscles flex as he moved his arms.

"I'll admit, I didn't think you would come," he confessed slyly, handing me my glass of wine. "I figured we'd be too much for you to handle."

Keeping my gaze on his, I took a sip of the wine and licked my lips. "Who knows, *I* might be the one who's too much to handle."

I hung my purse on the back of one the barstools while Ryley pulled out a chair for me at the kitchen table. As soon as I was seated, they both took their seats and smiled at me. My stomach growled, but it was also in knots.

I didn't like feeling nervous, but these guys made me that way. Slowly, I ate a few bites of my food, but it didn't help that they both kept watching me out of the corner of their eyes.

Finally, after we finished eating, they ushered me into the living room and I sat down on the couch while they took up the chairs opposite me. "I guess it's about time we get down to business," Ryley began.

Nodding, I sipped the last of my wine and set the glass down on the table beside the couch. "Tell me what you want."

Ryley and Camden both looked at each other and grinned before turning back to me. Camden was the one who spoke next, "Okay, like I told you in the car we both want you to ourselves. You had mentioned before that you don't do one night stands. In regards to that we want to offer you … more. That way it won't be considered a one night stand."

More what? I wondered.

"I see," I said. "Care to elaborate?"

Smirking, Camden moved closer so that his legs brushed up against mine. "What we want to offer is one night with each of us. Let us both have you to ourselves, and after that if you think you can handle us together, it'll be your choice. You can decide if you want the third night with us both, or if you want another night with just one of us. So, you see, it's not going to be a one night stand."

The proposition was actually kind of interesting, and my underwear was soaking wet just thinking about it. However, that couldn't be all they wanted. "What's the catch?" I asked. "Surely, there has to be something you're not telling me."

They both smiled again.

"Actually," Ryley started, "we don't exactly like a quick fuck. You have to be able to handle us for as long as we want to go. When we train before our fights, we need to keep our aggressions high, so we don't have sex during that time. Therefore, when we're finally able to let go of our urges, we want a little more flavor. If we want to tie you up, you need to let us. If you don't, then it's time to go; simple as that. If we don't like the way you kiss, we can let you go. I let a girl go last weekend because she liked to use her teeth while sucking my dick. It fucking hurt."

I bit my lip to keep from smiling. He probably deserved it.

"We won't force you into anything and we won't hurt you, but if you want to walk we immediately comply. All we crave is a little bit of fun."

"So if you prefer to fuck me in the ass I have to let you or it's all over?" I asked incredulously. The thought of getting screwed in the ass made me cringe. I knew of people who liked it, but I honestly had no desire to try it.

Both guys chuckled. "Yeah, if we wanted to, but that's not going to happen. I can see it in your face that you don't want that," Ryley added.

Blowing out a relieved sigh, I nodded and sat back on the couch, getting comfortable. "What about condoms? Do you wear them?"

They nodded, which was good because if they didn't, I was going to make them or the deal was off. There was no way I would have unprotected sex with them—or anyone for that matter—after the amount of women they'd been with.

"Is there anything else you'd like to know?" Camden asked.

Moving closer to him, I bit my lip and smiled. It was now time for my little game. "Actually, there is. What if you can't handle me? What if I don't like the way *you* kiss or the way you move during sex? What if you don't get me off? I think if you don't pass *my* test, I should have the option of letting *you* both go. It's not always about what *you* want, you know."

Ryley and Camden lifted their brows, intrigued. "Damn girl, I'm getting hard just thinking about this," Ryley chimed. "Please go on."

If they could mess with me, I was going to mess with them. Placing my hands on their thighs, I massaged them gently, slowly inching up the inside of their legs. They both groaned and moved closer.

"I know you get to do whatever you want with me, but what do you say about letting me do whatever I want with you? For one hour of the night, I want to be able to have all control, and that means whatever I do you have to let me do it, no questions asked. During that time you can't get off no matter what. If you do, I can walk away knowing full well that I bested you."

They stared at me for a few minutes, grinning from

ear to ear, while I sat there with an arrogant smirk on my face. I knew they didn't think I could wear them down, but I had full confidence that I could.

"I'm down for it," Ryley agreed. "No woman has ever been able to control me like that."

"Same here," Camden said.

Biting my lip, I nodded my head and removed my hands from their thighs. They were both hard, straining against their jeans, and from what I could tell they weren't exactly lacking in the size department. Hopefully I'd be able to walk after they were done with me.

Abruptly, I stood, making them shift back in their seats. "All right, you're on. When does all of this begin?"

"Friday night, angel," Ryley explained. "We don't have any fights this weekend, so it's the perfect time to have you all to ourselves."

"Who gets me first?" I asked curiously. "If you both want me, how do you decide who gets the privilege of breaking me in?"

Gazes dark, they tensed and glared at each other for a moment before turning back to me. "That's where we're going to have a problem," Camden growled. "We both want you first, so we decided it would only be fair for you to choose. Better yet, we'll fight for you. Do *you* have a preference on who you want first?"

Okay, that didn't put me on the spot or anything. Were they really going to fight for me? Expectantly, they both stared at me—their bodies ready for action—waiting on me to answer … but I didn't have one. I didn't want them to have to fight for me.

"Look, guys, I don't know you well enough to be able to pick between you. I'm sorry, but I can't choose. I don't want you fighting for me either."

The air in the room crackled like fire from the intense energy pouring off of their bodies. They smiled at each other before Ryley left the room, returning with two sets of handwraps and gloves.

Wrapping his hands, Ryley gazed at me and said, "Angel, I'm sorry, but there's no other choice. Either you pick between us or we fight."

Exasperated, I gazed at them wide-eyed with my mouth wide open. "You're going to fight now?"

Camden took off his shirt and smacked his fists together. "Why not? You do want to know who gets to feel that sweet body of yours first, don't you?"

"I do, but are you going to fight by the rules?" I asked.

Ryley tapped me on the chin with his gloved hand and winked. "We're not in the ring tonight, baby. Tonight we aren't fighting for money … we're fighting for you. There are no rules."

Ryley took my hand, leading me out the back door past the pool area, and Camden followed along beside me with his fists clenched at his sides. Just ahead there was a wide open garden with a white stone gazebo off to the side, surrounded by marble statues.

It reminded me of what I thought a garden in Roman times looked like; very medieval, but also kind of magical as the soft green grass shimmered in the moonlight from the dew.

Dropping his hand to the small of my back, Ryley gently pushed me up the steps of the gazebo and waltzed out to the middle of the garden with Camden. There were no rules tonight and that had me worried. I had never watched a fight with no rules, and if they weren't careful one of them could get really hurt.

They circled around the garden with their fists in defense mode, glaring at each other, ready to fight. "All right, angel," Ryley called. "This is how it's going to go down. Either we fight until we say it's over, or you call it for us. I'll go ahead and tell you it won't be good if you wait on us to call it."

"Great," I groaned sarcastically. "Not that that's any pressure or anything."

They both chuckled and shrugged their shoulders. "You had the choice, but you wanted it the hard way, sweetheart," Camden chimed. "Now you have to live with watching us beat the shit out of each other. On your command, we fight."

Taking a deep breath, I closed my eyes and yelled, "Fight!"

I might as well get it over with, right? Almost immediately, they started in on each other with jabs and striking combinations. The sound of their fists hitting flesh made me cringe, but I still kept my gaze on them, hoping it would be over soon. Why didn't I just pick one of them?

For about eight minutes they fought relentlessly—pounding on each other hard—until I couldn't take anymore. They weren't close to ending the fight, but I knew that if I didn't stop it they would be bruised and worthless by the weekend. Neither one of them had faltered and neither one of them were better than the other, but a decision needed to be made.

"Stop," I yelled. "I want you to stop!"

Breathing hard, their chests heaving up and down, they both backed away and leaned over on their knees, resting. "I'm sorry, but I can't watch this anymore. It's different when you're up against someone else, but fighting each other isn't easy to watch."

"Have you made a choice then?" Ryley asked. "We can't stop until you make your choice."

"Fine," I growled, throwing my hands up in the air. "I'm going to flip for it, and whoever the coin lands on will get me first." Running inside, I grabbed a penny out of my purse, and then rushed back out to join them on the grass. I flipped the coin and caught it in my palm, my hands covering the verdict.

"All right, guys. Ryley, you're heads, and Camden, you're tails."

Taking a deep breath, I closed my eyes and uncovered the penny, nervous and excited to finally find out who would get to be with me first. When I opened them, I got my answer.

CHAPTER II

Ashleigh

THE FIGHT WAS intense. Hopefully, the past four days was enough time to let them both heal from the brutal beating they bestowed upon each other. I couldn't believe they wanted to do that for me; it was actually kind of enthralling.

All week, Ryley and Camden had texted me numerous times about how they couldn't wait to be with me this weekend. Ryley's messages were more sexy and tasteful, whereas Camden's were vulgar and straight to the point. He even sent me pictures of his cock, which I found to be quite interesting. I'd nearly choked on a potato chip when I opened the message on my phone.

Gabriella didn't know what I had planned with the twins and I wanted to keep it that way for now. Announcing to everyone that I was about to have sex with two brothers wasn't exactly what I wanted to advertise to the world, especially to her and Colin.

For now, it would be my secret. Thankfully, Gabriella had already left to go out with Bradley, so I didn't have to worry about her seeing me leave with my date.

The doorbell rang promptly at six-thirty like I was told it would. All I knew was that I needed to be ready to go at that time with an overnight bag and dressed in something nice. I'd decided on one of my little skin tight black dresses with sexy black lingerie underneath, along with my garters and black stilettos. Since he wanted me dressed nicely, I had a feeling he was going to take me out to dinner somewhere before having his way with me for the rest of the night.

When I answered the door, my date for the evening stood there—leaning against the door frame—his blond hair perfectly gelled, and wearing a pair of black slacks and a midnight blue shirt that matched his eyes. Seeing him all dressed up, and his tattoos covered, I would never have pictured him as a hardcore UFC fighter.

"Are you ready?" he asked, holding out his hand.

As I'll ever be.

Taking his hand, I nodded and followed him out to the same car he'd picked me up in just a few nights ago. He looked hot as hell, although he still had a few light bruises on the left side of his face.

Thankfully I'd called the fight when I did; if not, he and his brother would be looking kind of rough right now. Camden was the one who ended up being the coin toss winner.

Once he helped me into his car, he bent down and

wrapped his hand around my neck, pulling me closer to his lips. I willingly complied, letting him open my mouth with his tongue so that he could taste me and caress my lips. The kiss was firm and demanding, but I wanted more. Before I could deepen the kiss, he pulled away with a smirk on his face.

"I wanted to do that the other night, but I never got the chance. We only have this one night, and I have to make it last before we run out of time."

As soon as he got in the car, we were on our way. "Where are we going?" I asked.

Reaching over to put a hand on my bare leg, he smiled and slid his hand higher up my thigh. "You'll see, sweetheart. Just sit back and enjoy the ride. The fun starts now."

His fingers slid up under my dress, and he immediately groaned when he touched me. "Fuck me," he growled. "You're not wearing any underwear." Shifting in his seat, he unbuckled his pants to give him more room, and sighed. "You know I'm not going to be able to think of anything else while we eat dinner, right?"

"Same goes for me," I chuckled. His thumb grazed along my clit and I gasped, gripping on to the edge of the seat. *Now I'm definitely not going to be able to think of anything else.*

"Open your legs up just a bit," he ordered gently. "I want to get you wet."

Doing as he instructed, I closed my eyes and laid my head against the seat. "I think you're a little late for that."

When his fingers found my opening, he cursed under his breath and groaned. "Shit, you're right. Do you want me that bad, or have you not been properly fucked in a while?"

Turning my head, I looked over at him with lazy, heat-filled eyes and bit my lip. "Both, actually. Although, Big Red takes care of me every once in a while."

"What's Big Red?" he asked with a curious glint in his eye. By the way his cock jumped in his pants he already knew the answer to that. I had never understood the fascination men had with women who pleasured themselves.

When he pushed his fingers inside of me, I gasped and opened my legs further. "I think you already know what I'm talking about," I moaned breathlessly.

He thrust his fingers faster, rubbing his thumb along my clit with the same speed. My orgasm came so fast it didn't even have time to build. Slamming my head against the seat, my eyes rolled back in my head as I screamed out my pleasure, rocking my hips against his hand.

"Oh my God, Camden, don't stop."

His deep chuckle resonated in my ear as he slowed his pace, waiting on the tremors to stop, and carefully pulled his fingers out of me. Slowly, he made sure my gaze was on him when he put his fingers in his mouth and sucked them off, breathing in the scent of me.

"You taste so fucking good. As soon as we get to the house, I'm going to carry you inside and lay you on the kitchen counter so I can really taste you."

Holy hell, I'm going to be in trouble ... and I can't wait. I wanted more already.

He drove faster along the highway, and since Malibu was only about forty-five minutes from Los Angeles, it didn't take us too long to get there. Especially since we spent over half of the time with him pleasuring me.

The house was amazingly beautiful, with windows all around, as if it were made of glass. As we pulled up, I could only imagine the view of the ocean from the backside.

Camden got out of the car first and came around to open my door. After helping me out, he shut it and immediately swept me up in his arms to carry me inside. "You were serious, weren't you?" I teased seductively.

"You're damn right, sweetheart."

The second he opened the door, the smell of rosemary and lemon pepper chicken made my mouth water. He carried me to the kitchen where a whole spread of food was laid out on the kitchen table, along with a selection of wines.

I didn't get to see much of it because Camden set me down and pulled me in tight against him before backing me up against the counter. His lips descended on mine as his hands found my waist, lifting me up.

Feverishly, he trailed his kisses down my neck to the mounds of my breasts while he lifted my dress above my hips. "I'm going to make you come so hard you're not going to think about anything else other than me tonight."

Gazing up into his heat-filled blue eyes, I leaned forward and bit his lip. "I think I can handle that," I murmured huskily.

Laying me down on the cold marble countertop and spreading me wide, he licked his lips and lowered his head to between my legs. My clit throbbed; even more so when his tongue flicked across it, making me gasp.

"I don't know, baby. You might not be able to handle me tonight. I'm going to make sure you can't walk after I'm done with you. I want my brother to know it was me who fucked you hard … not him."

In one quick movement, he thrust his fingers inside of me and closed his lips over my clit, sucking and licking. I gasped with the pleasure and pain of it all. "Fuck, you're so wet," he groaned. "I can feel you getting tighter. Am I that good, baby? Is my tongue driving you wild?"

Removing his fingers, he replaced them with his warm tongue and entered me, thrusting and rubbing my clit with his nose. The friction was mind-blowing, and along with his tongue I was about to lose control, especially when he gripped the inside of my thigh and growled. He knew I was close.

"I want you to come, baby. Let me taste how much I turn you on."

The moment my body exploded, I screamed out his name and rocked my hips until the last remnants of my orgasm subsided. Breathing hard, I laid there on the counter until Camden righted himself, took my hands, and helped me up. "Did that feel good?" he asked slyly, pressing his hard cock against my stomach.

"Better than good," I replied breathlessly. "It felt amazing."

"Good. Well, then let's enjoy our dinner before I rip every single thing you're wearing off of your body."

Taking my hand, he led me to the table and pulled out a chair for me. "Does that sound like a plan, Ashleigh?"

Just hearing him say my name gave me chills. I could only imagine what the rest of the night was going to be like, especially when I had my hour to do with him as I wished. After sitting down at the table, Camden pushed in my chair and pulled the cover off of my meal.

On the plate was rosemary chicken with garlic

mashed potatoes and buttered asparagus. It smelled amazing, and tasted even better than that when I took my first bite. I was starving and knew I would need my energy for the rest of the night.

I didn't know Camden well, but between him and his brother, he seemed darker, more mysterious, like there was something forbidden hidden beneath the surface. There was something in his eyes that screamed danger; I could see it when he gazed at me. In a way it made me nervous, but it was a good nervous ... an excited nervous.

Taking another bite of the chicken, I moaned and chewed it slowly; it was amazing. "Did you cook the food?"

There was no way he could have with the long drive we had to get out there.

"No, Ryley's the only one of us who can actually cook. I had someone come in and do it. Do you like it?"

"Yes, it's amazing," I gushed. "I'm a pretty good cook ... sometimes." It was easy throwing something in the oven or crock pot, but if I had to cook on the grill I was lost. We ate in silence for a few minutes, but after a while it started making me uncomfortable. I didn't like that awkward silence.

"So," I began, "have you ever been in love?"

Taking a bite of his food, Camden scoffed and shook his head. "No. Right now my life is perfect without having that useless emotion tainting it."

"I see," I said. "Sounds kind of lonely if you ask me."

"No, it's less complicated," he retorted. "What about you? Have you ever been in love?"

I nodded. "A couple of times, actually. It's kind of nice while it lasts."

"I think love makes people weak."

Either he actually believed that or it was just a front; I couldn't tell by the blank expression on his face. "What kinds of things do you like to do?" I asked. "Other than fighting and chasing women, of course."

He shrugged. "I like to surf when I get the chance. Sometimes it's hard with my training schedule, but usually I try to take a morning and go out to the coast."

"That sounds like fun. I've always wanted to learn how to surf." I paused for a second, thinking he would look up at me at least once, but he didn't. It was like talking to a brick wall. "So how did you and your brother get into fighting?"

Slowly, he lowered his fork and lifted his gaze, his lips in a flat line as if he was irritated. "Do you always ask this many questions?"

"Sometimes," I drawled out slowly. "Is there something wrong with asking how you started fighting?"

"No, it's just annoying and it takes up too much time. You need to eat so we can get this night going."

Uh ... what the hell just happened? It was like we were on a time clock, or better yet like talking to Dr. Jekyll and Mr. Hyde.

After we finished our dinner, I set my plate in the sink while Camden ventured off upstairs. He wouldn't tell me what he was doing or let me join him. *I wonder what his problem is.*

One minute he was fine, and the next it was like he was another person. While he was gone, I ventured into the living room, which was bathed in gold and pink hues from the sunset. It was beautiful as I stood there watching the waves through the back windows.

Fetching my phone from my purse to take a picture and send it to Gabriella, I noticed I had a text from Ryley.

Ryley: Think about me tonight. I know I'm thinking about you.

A smile lit up my face when I texted him back.

Me: It's kind of hard not to when you and your brother look exactly alike.

Ryley: Well, I wish you were with me. I'm going to spend the rest of the night pretending that my brother isn't fucking you. Be prepared for me tomorrow night. Sleep tight, angel.

Was it bad that I kind of wished I was with him and not Camden?

Me: Sweet dreams, Ryley.

Ryley: About you.

"Who are you texting?" Camden asked. "I have to say I'm a little jealous right now. You haven't smiled like that around me."

Nonchalantly, I put my phone back in my purse and waved him off. "Oh, it was just Ryley being silly, that's it."

As soon as I said it, I regretted it. His gaze darkened and his smile disappeared. "I see. Well, I guess I need to get your mind off of him, don't I?"

Roughly, he grabbed me around my waist and pulled me to him, kissing me hard while the stubble on his chin rubbed me raw. "Whoa … calm down," I gasped, putting my hands on his chest and backing away. "You're not mad, are you? I thought you and your brother liked to share."

"We do," he growled, "but it's never been with someone like you. You're different, and to see you smiling the way you were because of him and not me pisses me off. What is it about him that everyone likes?"

His grip on my waist tightened, but I kept my hands on his chest to hold him off. He was angry, but in his eyes I could see the true problem … he was jealous. Sibling rivalry was common and I was pretty sure with two twin alpha males it could get pretty lethal. I had no clue there was this much tension between them.

"Camden," I murmured softly. "I'm here with *you* to-night, not Ryley. So he texted me, big deal. There's noth-ing to get upset about. You've both texted me all week."

"Yeah, but he knows tonight is mine. He shouldn't be trying to mess with you while you're with me."

His gaze was so intense it started to make me uncom-fortable. I didn't want to be involved in a sibling rivalry battle, especially between two volatile men.

"That may be true," I admitted honestly. "He shouldn't be texting me, but I also think that instead of getting pissed off you should just get even. Tomorrow night when I'm with him, text me and I'll make sure to text you back in front of him."

"That's not going to do shit," he thundered. "It doesn't matter what's going on, he will always be the best; the one everyone wants."

Sliding my hands up his chest, I took his face in my hands and held him firm. "Hey, let's not spend this night talking about your brother. I'm with you tonight; I want you. How about we go outside and take a walk on the beach to clear your head. We can talk about it and get to know each other."

Camden grunted and jerked away. "What? I didn't bring you here to get to know you. And the last thing I want to do is talk about my issues with my brother. All you need to know about me is what I plan on doing to you tonight."

He completely moved away from my touch and headed into the kitchen where he fetched a bottle of wine from the refrigerator and uncorked it. Frozen in place, I couldn't help but wonder if he was just kidding with his last comment or if he was serious.

Surely, he wasn't that big of an asshole, right? Pouring two glasses of wine, he handed me one and then took a sip out of the other with a serious glint in his eyes.

"So ... you really don't have any interest in getting to know me at all, do you?" I asked.

Smugly, he downed his glass of wine and chuckled. "Honestly, no. You're hot, way hotter than any of the girls I've fucked, and the good thing is that I know you're not a whore. The last thing I want is a piece of ass that a thousand guys have already tainted."

Scoffing, I crossed my arms at the chest, completely at a loss for words other than to tell him to fuck off.

Camden rolled his eyes. "Oh, now don't be like that. I was trying to give you a compliment. All that matters tonight is that you want to fuck me and I want to fuck you. That's the deal, right? That's all you're here for."

"How do you know that's all I'm here for?" I asked. "Maybe I thought it would be nice to get to know you before we spend the whole night having sex. I like to talk to the guys I have sex with."

"Well, I have no interest in that, sweetheart. Besides, you didn't seem to be doing much talking when I had you spread out over the kitchen counter."

Mouth gaping open, I stood there stunned, completely taken aback with his shift in mood. Yeah, okay, so I did decide to spend the night with him, but I was under the impression that it would be something different ... something more. He started off so sweet and seductive, but now he was an arrogant bastard. I didn't like it one bit.

Strolling toward the stairs, Camden waved for me to follow him, as if I was dog who needed to obey its master. When I didn't follow him, he glanced at me over his shoulder, his eyebrows raised. "Are you coming?"

"Of course," I replied, smiling from ear to ear. "Go on up and I'll be right there. I'm going to get myself another glass of wine."

"Okay, but hurry up."

As soon as he was up the stairs, I pulled out my phone and saw I had about three text messages from Ryley. Not taking the time to look at them, I searched for the number I needed and dialed it, knowing I needed to hurry. My time with Camden was up.

CHAPTER

12

Ryley

I TEXTED ASHLEIGH several more times and never received a reply back. Either she was tired of me sending her messages or she was busy with my brother. It sucked that he got her first, but then again, she saved the best for last.

I was going to be the last one to touch her, she would remember *me,* and I was going to make sure she did. That was what made my brother and me different. He would try to seduce his way inside of her, but I had other plans.

Picking up my phone, I dialed Gabriella's number and waited on her to pick up. When she did, she was already expecting for something to be wrong. "You better not be in any trouble," she answered as a way of greeting.

I chuckled. "No, I'm actually at home watching TV. I have some questions for you. Can you talk?"

"Well, I'm kind of on a date, but if you make it quick I'll see if I can help you."

"What kinds of things does Ashleigh like to do for fun?" I asked.

The line went quiet for a second, and then Gabriella sighed. "Ryley, what are you up to? She already told you she's not interested. I swear you and your brother are so damn stubborn."

"It runs in the family," I joked. "But please, tell me the things she likes to do."

"Okay, fine ... let's see." She briefly paused. "She loves to play tennis, go hiking, white water rafting, and believe it or not ... fishing. Her family lives in Colorado, so she loves the mountains and anything outdoors. Her favorite movie is *The Ugly Truth*, and her absolute favorite treat are those Dove chocolates that are swirled with mint. I think she's addicted to them."

She actually sounded pretty interesting. I'd never met an outdoor type of girl.

"Thanks, Gabby. What about food? What's her favorite meal?"

"Uh, let's see. Her favorite right now is grilled salmon. She gets it all the time when we go out to eat at the pub across the street from our apartment. It always comes with a black bean cake and fried zucchini."

That was definitely doable.

"Thank you, Gabby," I remarked appreciatively. "I think I have everything I need."

"You're welcome, Ryley. Do you plan on sharing this stuff with your brother?" she asked.

"Hell no, he should've been smart enough to call you on his own. I'll let him fail on this one."

"You are so bad, Mr. Jameson. I hope this helps you, although, I'm going to be honest, I don't think it will. Good luck."

"Thanks."

We both hung up, and I already had my game plan set. Ashleigh wanted me to remember her … well, I wanted her to remember me. My date was going to be one she wouldn't forget.

CHAPTER

18

Ashleigh

I HAD FIFTEEN minutes to do what I needed to do and get the hell out of there. As much as I wanted to like Camden, I just couldn't do it. Quickly, I rushed up the stairs and down the hallway until I found him, in a dark room all covered in shades of blue, lounging completely naked across a king size bed. There were also ropes dangling from the bed posts … perfect. I loved being tied up, but this time it wasn't going to be me.

"Wow, you don't want to waste time, do you?"

Licking his lips, he smiled and shook his head. "We don't have the time to waste. Come here," he demanded.

I did as he said and waltzed over to him, only to have him lift me onto the bed and cover me with his body. His cock was hard, pressing in between my legs as he leaned down and feverishly kissed me.

Opening my lips, I let him taste me and touch me all over my body. It felt good, but I knew I had to sacrifice my own pleasures for the greater good of the situation.

"Lay back on the bed," I commanded. "I want my hour."

"Are you sure you don't want me to play with you for a while?" he asked, thrusting his hips against mine.

I bit his bottom lip and sucked on it before letting go. "Nope, I'm ready now. You remember the rules, don't you?"

He chuckled and slid off of me so he could lie down on the bed. "I sure do. Your hour starts now." Reaching for his phone, he started up the timer and it began to count down. "Where do you want me?" he asked.

Smiling, I bit my lip and straddled his waist, gazing mischievously at the silk ropes he had tied to the posts. "I'm assuming you planned on using those on me?" I inquired, pointing to the ropes.

His lip tilted up in a smirk. "What can I say? I want you completely at my mercy."

"Well, right now you're going to be completely at mine. Lie down and lift your arms above your head," I demanded.

Licking his lips, he groaned and did as I said. I smiled because I knew that smug look on his face wasn't going to last long. Taking the smooth, black silk ropes, I bound his wrists tightly to each post, and also his feet to the ones at the edge of the bed. The last thing I wanted was for it to be easy for him to get out of them when I needed to do what I needed to do.

Now that he was tied up, I reached behind my back

and unzipped my dress so that I could lift it over my head. Camden whistled when he saw the black lingerie underneath, along with my black garters and crotchless underwear.

"You like it?" I asked.

He pulled against his restraints like he wanted to touch me, but couldn't. "Fuck yeah, I do. What are you going to do to me now?"

Glancing at his phone, I noticed that five minutes had already passed. *Let him have it*, I thought to myself. "Right now, I want you to close your eyes and lay your head back. Relax."

When he complied, I slid off to his side and wrapped one of my legs around his so I could open him up further. His cock was rock hard and lying against his stomach when I reached for it, gripping him tight at the base. He trembled when I began to pump his length, up and down while cupping his balls and massaging them.

"Does that feel good?" I asked breathlessly.

"Hmm ... it would feel better if you sucked my cock."

I rolled my eyes. "All in good time, baby. This is my hour, remember? You get what I give you."

If there was anything I learned during the time I dated my ex-boyfriend, it was how to get him off quickly if we were in a rush for a quickie. However, with Camden I had to do it slightly different; I didn't want to have sex with him to do it.

Straddling his waist cowgirl style, I used my hand to pump him and brought my other one to my lips so I could lubricate my fingers with my saliva.

Slowly, I massaged his balls and gently slipped a fingertip inside of his ass. "What the fuck are you doing?" he gasped, lifting his head.

I glanced back at him over my shoulder and smiled innocently. "What does it feel like I'm doing? You can't tell me that with all of the women you've been with no one has ever done this to you."

Gently, I pushed my finger back in and thrust it forward while squeezing his cock harder. He trembled and let his head fall back on the bed, groaning. "Holy fuck that feels so good."

What he didn't know was that if I put just a little more pressure …

He tensed underneath me and I knew he was close to losing it. I had only been working him ten minutes when his strangled cry echoed through the room. "Ashleigh, slow down!"

It was too late; I knew I had him. He released hot and swift as I slowly milked him the rest of the way while pressing on that sensitive spot inside of his ass. Breathing hard, his eyes were closed and his chest heaved up and down, glistening with sweat in the candlelight.

"I believe that took all of ten minutes," I boasted triumphantly. Climbing off of his body, I rolled from the bed and pulled my dress back on.

"How the hell did you do that?" he asked, finally opening his eyes to look at me. When he noticed me zipping up my dress, he furrowed his brows and tried to get up … but couldn't.

"Untie me, Ashleigh. That was unfair and you know it."

Innocently, I smiled. "I have no clue what you're talking about. You were the one who thought you'd be able to handle me for an hour."

Struggling against the restraints, his face turned blood red. "Fine, you won. Now untie me before I really get pissed off."

"But the hour isn't up yet, Cam. Maybe next time you'll think twice about underestimating what a woman can do. I think a lesson in humility will do you some good."

Turning on my heel, I stalked out of the room and went straight to the bathroom to wash up. Camden yelled for me to come back, but I kept walking, ignoring his angry shouts. Hopefully, the cab I called was still outside waiting for me.

"Goddammit, Ashleigh, get back here!"

Knowing I couldn't leave him there like that, I stopped at the front door and dialed Ryley's number. I knew Camden was going to hate me after what I did, and honestly I didn't care. It wasn't like he meant anything to me anyway. Maybe he'd start to rethink the way he treated women.

Yeah, right, I highly doubt that.

At least he would remember me as being the girl that fucked him over. I was stupid for agreeing to their messed up arrangement in the first place. If Ryley was anything like Camden, I didn't want any part of it. Ryley's phone kept ringing, and I was about to hang up when he finally answered.

"Should you be calling me right now?" he asked teasingly.

"Actually, no, but I need you to drive to Malibu and help your brother."

"What happened? Is he okay?"

Camden was shouting so loud in the background that I knew Ryley could hear him over the phone. "Uh … well, he's okay physically. Maybe just a little tied up, but I think his ego might be bruised a bit."

Ryley chuckled. "I'm on my way. Are you leaving him right now? How are you getting back home?"

Opening the door, I saw the cab at the edge of the driveway, waiting. "Yes, I'm leaving. I called a cab. Listen, he's not happy, so be prepared."

The sound of his car engine rumbled through the phone. "What did you do to him? You're not going to do the same to me are you?"

Before getting into the cab, I stopped in the middle of the driveway and looked back up at the house. "Ryley, listen, I knew what I was getting into when I agreed to these nights. No, I didn't expect you to fall in love with me or to date me, believe me, that's the last thing I want. I have no interest in that. All Camden had to do was play nice and be somewhat of a gentleman. When he didn't do that, he paid the price. Honestly, I don't see how Gabriella thinks so highly of you two."

"Whoa … hang on a second. What did he do or say to you to get you so pissed off?"

The cab driver honked the horn, so I jerked around and started toward him, hoping he wouldn't leave. "Look, it doesn't matter what he said; I'm done. You both can kiss my ass."

Hanging up the phone, I immediately turned it off and hopped into the cab. The driver was a middle-aged man with greasy salt and peppered hair and a scruffy beard. The cab smelled like stale smoke and body odor, but I choked back the bile in my throat and apologized, "I'm so sorry, sir. Thank you for waiting on me." I told him my address and slid him fifty dollars. "Here's fifty to start off with. I'll pay you more as soon as you get me home."

I was ready to get out of there and forget that any of it happened.

CHAPTER 14

Ryley

I TRIED CALLING Ashleigh back, but her phone went straight to voicemail. Knowing my brother, I could only imagine the stupid shit he must've said to piss her off. Whatever she did to him, I was pretty sure he deserved it. There were times when I wanted to lay into him for the way he treated people, especially women. He wasn't exactly known for his smooth words.

When I pulled up to the house, I rushed out of my car and straight through the front door. "Cam," I shouted, "where are you?"

"You have got to be fucking kidding me," he growled from the second floor.

Rushing up the stairs, I found him in one of the bedrooms, face red with rage and tied to the bed ... completely naked. Eyes wide, I put my hand over my mouth to hide my smile. "Yeah, that's right, laugh it up," he hissed. "Get me the fuck out of here."

"I will, but first tell me what happened. Ashleigh called me to come get you. What did you do to her?"

"Oh, fuck that bitch," he shouted. "You better not be hooking up with her tomorrow. This same shit will happen to you."

I highly doubted that because I wouldn't have been stupid enough to let her tie me up; it would've been a deal breaker. "You don't have to worry about that," I told him. "She told me that we could both kiss her ass. She's done. Now what did you do to her?"

"Not a damn thing other than call her annoying because she kept asking me questions. I didn't bring her here to talk to her. I brought her to fuck her."

That was his mistake right there. You couldn't treat a girl like Ashleigh in that way and not have her retaliate. She was out of our league and I knew it, but I also knew how to play her ... he didn't.

"And did you ... fuck her?" I asked. He'd gotten off somehow; his body was covered in his come.

Clenching his teeth, he closed his eyes and huffed. "No, I didn't. Now untie me. I can't feel my damn hands."

As soon as I had him untied, he jumped off the bed, heading straight to the bathroom and into the shower. I had a feeling that wasn't all that happened, and if Camden wasn't going to tell me I had no other choice but to go to Ashleigh herself.

Before leaving to head back to Los Angeles, I waited downstairs for Camden to finish up his shower and get dressed because I wanted to see if I could get any more information from him. Unfortunately, he was still seething when he thundered down the steps.

"She must have really done a job on you," I said. "I don't think I've ever seen you this pissed off at a girl. She's probably going to tell Gabriella what happened, so you might as well tell me and get it over with."

"Who cares? I don't give a shit what she tells Gabriella."

"You should," I snapped. "Gabriella is our friend."

Camden poured himself a tumbler of whiskey from the bar and scoffed. "Gabriella is *your* friend. She doesn't care about hanging out with me. It's all you. You're the one everybody would rather be with. Even Ashleigh wanted you more than me."

Now that pissed me off.

"Really? That's what this is about? Did you ever stop to think that maybe she would've wanted you if you weren't such an asshole?"

"Whatever, Ryley," he backfired. "I have *never* had to work for a piece of ass, and I don't plan on starting any time soon."

"Well, if that's how you want to be, fine. However, I'm not going to let you drag me down with you." Turning on my heel, I marched to the door and opened it wide.

"Where are you going?" Camden shouted, following along behind me. "You're going to her, aren't you?"

When I got out to my car, I opened my door and glared at him. "Yes, I'm going to her. I don't want her thinking I'm anything like you."

"But you are! You're worse than me!"

"Maybe before," I said, getting into my car, "but not this time."

I needed to make things right.

CHAPTER 15

Ashleigh

IT WAS STILL early in the night when I made it home. There were no lights on in the apartment, so thankfully I'd be alone for a while until Gabriella made it back from her date. I had no idea how I was going to tell her about Camden. Maybe I shouldn't even bother. The last thing I wanted was to cause friction between her and her friends. I knew she loved them.

Once up the three flights of stairs, I unlocked the door and went straight to my room. I desperately wanted to change out of my dress and in to a pair of silky blue pajama pants and a white tank top.

By now, Camden was probably free and cursing me from one side of the world to the next. However, I didn't care. He deserved it and I wasn't going to feel bad about it.

In fact, I was going to celebrate my triumph with my favorite ice cream and a movie.

In the freezer, we had several pints … and one in particular was screaming my name as soon as I opened the door. Nothing could beat Ben & Jerry's Halfbaked with its chunks of brownies and cookie dough; not even my orgasm tonight could compare.

Once I had my spoon in hand, DVD in the player, and a blanket, I was all good to go. The instant I turned on the movie, there was a knock at the door and I instantly froze. Camden immediately came to mind, and I hoped like hell that I'd remembered to lock the door behind me when I got in.

Another knock came, but it didn't sound like it was someone who was pissed off. Quietly, I tiptoed to the door and peeked through the hole … it was Colin. His platinum blond hair was gelled into messy spikes and he wore a snug green T-shirt with his favorite pair of ripped denim jeans. Breathing a sigh of relief, I opened the door wide and smiled.

"Hey, what are you doing here?"

Gazing down at my pajamas, he smiled and walked in. "Well, I tried calling you to see if you wanted to hang out tonight, but your phone kept sending me to voicemail. You're not avoiding me, are you?"

"No, of course not," I gasped, shutting the door. This time I definitely made sure to lock it. "I turned my phone off a little while ago. Do you want some ice cream? I was about to watch a movie."

Once in the living room, he glanced over at the TV and back to me with an amused smirk on his face. "Let me guess … it's either going to be *Pitch Perfect* or *The Ugly*

Truth. Which one are we watching tonight?"

He followed me into the kitchen and I opened the freezer, letting him pick his own pint. He chose the peanut butter cup ice cream just like I knew he would. "I was going to watch *Pitch Perfect*. I need something that'll make me laugh."

We sat down on the couch and he bumped me with his shoulder. "Everything okay? You usually don't sit by yourself with ice cream and a movie unless something's bothering you. The last time you did it was when you and your ex broke up. What's going on now?"

Opening my pint, I stuck my spoon inside and paused before lifting it to my lips. "It's just been a long night," I told him.

He put his arm around me and squeezed. "Okay, I get it. You don't want to tell me. If you change your mind, I'm here."

"Thanks, Colin. It's just not something I feel comfortable talking to you about."

Kissing me on the head, he squeezed me one more time before reaching for his ice cream. "I understand, babe. Now turn on the movie so it'll make you feel better."

I pressed play and fast forwarded through the introduction stuff. "When are you going to go home and visit your family ... and your girlfriend?" I asked.

When he didn't answer, I looked over at him, taking in his weary gaze and furrowed my brows. "Colin? What's wrong?"

"I'm going to see them next weekend. I've been trying to get in touch with Erin all day. She's avoiding me and I don't know why. The last time we talked, she was preoccupied with something like she didn't really want to talk to me."

Erin was his girlfriend and had been for going on three years. "Everything was fine a couple of weeks ago when you saw her, wasn't it?" I asked.

"Yeah, as far as I could tell. I don't know, things have been kind of different lately."

"How so?"

Licking his lips, he turned his green gaze to mine and started to tell me when a loud knock came at the door. Now that knock had my stomach instantly tightening into knots.

"Who is that?" Colin asked, glancing back at the door.

My heart pounded and my palms began to sweat. "I don't know, but I'm sure they'll go away if we just ignore them."

The movie had started, so I kept my gaze on the TV; unfortunately, Colin kept his on mine. It didn't help that another loud knock came at the door. "Ashleigh, open the door," a voice called out. "It's Ryley."

Sighing, I closed my eyes and hung my head. "Dammit," I murmured low.

"What's he doing here?" Colin asked.

"I don't know exactly, but if his brother is out there it's not going to be good."

"Why? What happened?" When I wouldn't answer, he growled and got up to go to answer the door.

"Colin, no," I hissed. "Don't answer it."

Instead of listening to me, he opened the door and stood there like an avenging angel. It made me realize how much I loved having him in my life. He was a good friend … even if he didn't listen to me.

"Can I help you with something?" Colin snapped, his voice stony and hard.

Ryley's voice wasn't angry or bitter when he answered, "Yes, I'd like to speak to Ashleigh. I know she doesn't want to see me, but I need her to talk to me for just a minute."

Colin glanced back at me, lifting his eyebrows.

"Please, Ashleigh," Ryley called out. "I promise it'll only take a minute."

Setting my ice cream down, I huffed and got to my feet. "Fine."

Colin moved over a step so I could join him at the door, but stayed close. He kept his arm protectively behind me as he held the door, and it didn't go unnoticed by Ryley, who watched with narrowed eyes.

His blond hair was disheveled like he'd just woken up, and I had to admit it was kind of sexy along with his tight white T-shirt and tattoos down his right arm. However, his crystal blue eyes were nothing like his brother's tonight; they were full of concern, apologetic.

"Can we talk out here ... alone," he asked, pinning a glare at Colin.

"Where's Camden?"

"He's still in Malibu, or at least that's where I left him. He's not going to come here if that's what you're afraid of."

"Ashleigh, what's going on?" Colin asked, cutting in. "Do you need me to stay with you tonight?"

Ryley rolled his eyes, but kept his gaze on mine. "I'm sure she'll be fine. My brother isn't going to do anything stupid other than what he's already done."

Colin tensed behind me, but I turned around and put

my hand on his chest. "Everything's fine, Colin, I promise. Just give me one minute with Ryley and I'll be right back in, okay?"

Clenching his teeth, he huffed and glared at Ryley before slowly backing up with a warning in his gaze. As soon as he shut the door, Ryley moved closer. "Before you start bitching at me, I want you to hear me out."

"What do you want, Ryley?" I asked, stepping away. "I have nothing to say to you or Camden. I just want you to leave me alone. It was a mistake to get involved with you two."

"That's not true. I'm not going to apologize for my brother because frankly he's a dick. I thought he was going to be different with you, but I can see now that he wasn't."

"You think? I don't understand how you both get women treating them like dogs. I can handle being at the mercy of a dominant, but I *cannot* and will not be with someone who doesn't respect me. Hopefully, Camden realized tonight that I'm not an inferior in the bedroom."

Ryley bit his lip and lowered his gaze. "Yeah, about that ... how did you get him to blow his load? He wouldn't tell me what you did. I think that pissed him off more than anything."

"Well, he deserved it. A little anal action was all it took."

"Are you serious?" Ryley asked, eyes wide.

I held up my hands, feigning innocence. "Hey, it serves him right for being a complete and utter dick."

"So that's why you wanted an hour to do what you wanted with us. Well, I guess it's a good thing I don't have to worry about that anymore."

"I guess so," I snapped back.

We stared at each other in silence, neither one of us knowing what to say. Finally, Ryley nodded his head and slowly turned around. He started in the direction of the stairs, but then abruptly came back and grabbed my arms, not accepting defeat.

"Okay, look, I know you're not going to believe me, but I'm not like my brother." When I lifted my brows in disbelief, he paused and huffed, "Fine, maybe I am, but not in the ways you think. Let me prove to you that I'm not. I still want us to have *our* time together. Believe me, I had a whole day planned that didn't involve just sex. It was going to be a date, my first one actually."

"You're kidding me, right?"

"No," he replied in all seriousness. "I've never gone on a date and done things other than drinking, fucking, or fighting. It'll be a first for me."

"Why are you even doing this? There's nothing in it for you."

Slowly, he smiled and leaned over to kiss me on the cheek. "That's where you're wrong. There's always a first time for everything, right? It might actually be fun. I wouldn't know."

"And if it's not fun?" I asked. "Are you going to go back to being the inconsiderate ass who likes to gangbang chicks with his brother?"

Guffawing, Ryley turned on his heel and started toward the stairs. "Most likely, but if it's something I enjoy doing, I might have to consider a lifestyle change. However, it's all up to you. If you want me to be a better man, let me pick you up tomorrow. If you agree, I'll be here at ten in the morning."

"Ten? Why so early?"

"Why not? I told you I had the day planned." He started to descend the stairs backwards, smiling up at me as he went. "So what's your answer, angel? Are you going to give me this chance to make things right?"

Staring down at him, I rolled my eyes and sighed. "Fine, I'm in, but the first second you turn into a jackass I'm out. Take lessons from your brother … I don't play around."

He chuckled. "That's for damn sure. Just as long as you stay away from my ass we're fine." When he was completely off the stairs, I watched him walk toward his black Mercedes G600 in the parking lot. "I'll see you in the morning, sunshine," he called out over his shoulder.

Taking a deep breath, I waved at him once and watched him get in his car and leave. Either I'd just made the right decision, or possibly one of the worst ever by agreeing to the date with him.

I guess I'll find out tomorrow.

"Are you okay out here?" Colin asked, opening the door. He glanced around for Ryley, and when he didn't see him he stepped out to join me, crossing his arms over his chest. "So what did he want?"

"He asked me to go on a date with him tomorrow."

Colin nodded and looked away. "And I'm assuming you told him yes?"

"Yes, and I'm hoping I don't regret it."

"Are you going to tell me what happened with his brother or not? Is that where you were earlier … with him?"

When he lifted his green gaze to mine, I groaned and turned my face away. "Yeah," I answered sheepishly. "I kind of tied him to a bed and left him there."

"What?" he snapped. "You weren't going to fuck him, were you?"

"Well," I started nervously, "that was the plan until he started being a complete dick. When I saw an opportunity arise, I took it and left him there to suffer. Afterwards, I called Ryley and told him so that he could go there and untie him."

Putting his arm around my shoulder, he led me back inside. "You should have just left him there."

"True, but I'm not that cruel. I'm pretty sure he's embarrassed after what I did."

"Do you think he's pissed off enough to come by here tonight?" he asked, shutting the door.

"I don't think so, but then again, I don't know him that well. I really hope he doesn't." When I sat down on the couch, my ice cream wasn't on the table where I'd left it.

Smirking, Colin went to the freezer, pulling out our pints, and joined me on the couch. "I knew you would be out there longer than one minute. I didn't want them to melt, so I put these back."

"Aww ... thanks," I gushed, ignoring the way my heart felt when it fluttered. "I don't know what I'm going to do without you when we all graduate and go our separate ways."

"Well, it's a good thing we don't have to think about that right now. Do you mind if I stay here tonight?"

Snuggling up to his side, I turned the movie back on and smiled. "You don't even have to ask," I said softly. "You're always welcome to stay."

In that moment, I knew exactly what I wanted in life, but it was something I couldn't have.

CHAPTER 16

Ashleigh

THE NEXT MORNING, the sun shining brightly through the blinds, a text came through my phone, waking me up. However, it wasn't just me it woke up. Colin's raspy moan, along with his bare chest was all I could see and feel as I opened my eyes wide. I must've fallen asleep on the couch with him.

"Good morning," he murmured sleepily.

Bolting up, I slid off of the couch and grabbed my phone. It was nine o'clock in the morning. *Holy shit, I have to hurry.*

"What time did I fall asleep last night?" I asked. "I don't even remember."

He shrugged and put his hands behind his head, sprawling out now that I was off the couch. "I don't know, maybe a little after midnight."

"Why didn't you wake me up? It couldn't have been comfortable for you."

"Oh, he was fine," Gabriella chimed, waltzing into the room and winking at Colin. "Weren't you, Colin?"

Clearing his throat, he quickly glanced at me before reaching for his shirt and sliding it over his head. Colin had tattoos, but unlike Ryley and Camden, his didn't go down his arms. He had a dragon on his back, which curled around his biceps. I was with him when he got it; in fact, I had the privilege of helping him design it. He was a graphic artist and promised to design me a tattoo when I worked up the courage to get one.

"I guess need to get going so you can get ready for your date," he remarked dryly. "Call me later, Ash."

Quickly, he sent a warning glare to Gabriella before heading straight for the door and leaving. What was that all about?

"You have a date today?" Gabriella asked innocently. "Who with?"

"Ryley," I answered, looking down at the text he'd just sent.

Ryley: Be there in an hour.

"He says he's going to be here in an hour, so I probably need to get my ass in gear and get ready." Nodding, with an amused smirk on her face, she strolled into the kitchen to make her morning coffee. "What's that look for?" I asked. "You have a good time last night or something?"

"Actually, yeah, I did. Bradley and I had a good

night, but that's not why I'm smiling."

"Then why are you?"

"Because … I got a phone call last night from a very distraught friend of mine. Needless to say, I think it's pretty epic. Just don't leave my Ryley like that. He's the good one of the duo."

I gasped. "Camden actually called you? What did he say?"

"Well, he was kind of drunk and angry, so most of it I couldn't understand, but I did get the part where you tied him to the bed and left him. He must've really pissed you off for you to do that."

"Ugh … you have no idea. He deserved it, Gabby."

"Oh, I have no doubt. Camden is a real piece of work. I don't talk to him as much as I do his brother. He just doesn't have a warm personality like Ryley does."

"Yes, I know," I said, glancing down at my phone. "I told Ryley to stay away from me, but he showed up here anyway last night and promised he was different from his brother. He wants to spend the day with me, and I have no idea why I said yes."

"I know why," she marveled. "It's because he's hot, single, and something that can distract your mind from a certain someone else who's taken already. Not to mention he's every girl's fantasy come to life. Go and enjoy it. What do you have to lose?"

Nothing, I thought to myself. *I have nothing to lose.* Suddenly, what she'd said registered.

"Wait, what do you mean from someone else? There is no one else," I snapped incredulously.

Shaking her head in disbelief, she rolled her eyes at me. "Okay, keep telling yourself that. How long have you had a thing for Colin? You were snuggled up nice and tight with him last night when I got home."

Waving her off, I marched off down the hallway to my room. "I don't have a thing for Colin," I called out. "He has a girlfriend, and I've known that for the past two years. Besides, I'm getting ready to go out with Ryley and have wild monkey sex with him."

I wasn't planning on it, but I'd say anything to get her off my back. Colin was my friend and that's all he ever would be; I'd known that for a long time now.

Gabriella burst out laughing. "Yeah, you do that. Let me know how it goes."

Barely controlling my own giggles, I shut the door to my room and rushed to the bathroom so I could take a quick shower. While the water got warm, I fired up my laptop and let my favorite soundtracks play over the speakers. "Classic" by MKTO was my ultimate favorite song at the moment, so I put it on repeat before I hopped under the running water.

I hummed along with the song, dancing around the shower while I quickly washed my hair and body, hoping I could shave before running out of time. After everything that had happened yesterday, I needed to wash every trace of Camden off my body. By the fourth run of my song, I figured it was way past time to get out of the shower and get moving.

The room was so steamy I could barely see, and I loved breathing in the raspberry scent of my shampoo and body wash. Smiling, I took a deep breath and opened the shower door, only to be startled by a set of hypnotic blue eyes staring amusingly up and down my body, and holding a towel in his hands.

117

Shrieking, I stepped back and started to slip, but Ryley jumped forward and wrapped his arms around my bare body, steadying me. "Damn, I must say you look incredibly sexy right now," he murmured.

Pushing him off, I snatched the towel out of his hand and quickly wrapped it around my body. "What the hell are you doing coming in here like this? Not to mention you're early."

Amused, he grinned wide and leaned against the door frame. "Gabriella let me in, so I thought I would wait for you in your room. I must say, it was too tempting not to come in here with you. You have a beautiful voice, by the way."

"Thanks," I said, rolling my eyes. "How long have you been here? You just texted me about ten minutes ago saying you would be here in an hour."

"Yeah, about that, I was actually outside in the parking lot. I got to see your friend leave looking none too happy. I guess he wasn't thrilled when you told him you were going out with me, huh?"

"Not exactly, but it's not like it matters anyway … he's just a little overprotective."

"Isn't that a little much for someone who's just a friend?"

I shrugged. "It's just the way he is. I make my own choices."

Ryley moved closer and brushed the wet hair off my shoulders before tilting my chin up with his fingers. "Ah, I think I get it now. Well, the poor fool doesn't know what he's missing, does he?"

"I guess not," I confessed.

Taking my hand, Ryley smiled and led me out of the

bathroom. "All right, angel, hurry up and get dressed. We're going to have some fun today and I'm going to do everything I can to make sure you think about me and not your friend. Are you okay with that?"

He sat down on my bed, all confident and sexy in a pair of khaki shorts and a navy Oakley T-shirt with his gorgeous blue eyes staring back at me. Was I okay with him helping me forget? If he could prove he was different from his brother, I would certainly let him try.

"All right," I agreed.

Biting his lip, he stood up and came straight to me, grasping my cheeks in his large, warm hands. "That's all I needed to hear."

The next thing I knew his lips were on mine and he held me firm, caressing my cheeks with his thumbs as he kissed me. He smelled so amazingly good—thanks to whatever cologne he had put on—that I moved closer and breathed him in. Camden definitely didn't kiss like Ryley.

"Wow, okay," I panted, breaking the kiss. Ryley smirked and licked his lips, taking a step back. "Let me get dressed and then we can go. Getting out of this room is definitely a necessity."

He chuckled and sat back down on the bed. "And why is that? Are you afraid of what could happen?"

Rushing to my closet, I pulled out a tank top and a pair of denim shorts. "Yes, that's exactly what I'm saying. You're too dangerous to be alone with."

Shaking his head with his usual amused smirk on his face, he got up and went to the door. "Fine, I'll wait for you in the living room. You might want to pack some extra clothes, such as a bathing suit, and maybe some old ones that you wouldn't mind getting dirty."

"Dirty? What exactly are we going to do? Play in the mud?" I teased.

He winked. "Not exactly, but then again I'm new to all of this. I'm going to do something with you that I've never done with another female. Frankly, none of them would be up for it. You, on the other hand, I think would enjoy it. Or at least, I hope you do."

Opening the door, he smiled at me one last time before walking out and shutting it behind him. I could still feel his kiss on my lips, causing me to tremble all the way down throughout my body. If he kept that up, I was going to be in some serious trouble by the end of the day. What the hell was I talking about ... I was already in trouble.

CHAPTER 17

Ashleigh

GABRIELLA WAS TALKING to Ryley while loading up a small cooler with drinks when I made it into the kitchen, my overnight bag draped across my shoulder. Since he'd been talking about getting dirty, I didn't even bother with makeup or fixing my hair. I ran my hair dryer through it for a minute, and then braided it down the side in a Katniss-style braid.

"Wow, I think this is a world record," Gabriella teased. "It didn't take you long at all to get ready."

Ryley winked. "It's because she was in a hurry to get back to me."

"Please," I scoffed. "Keep telling yourself that. Are you ready to go?"

"I've been waiting on *you*, angel," he said, getting up

from the bar stool.

Squealing, Gabriella handed him the cooler. "Oh, you two are so cute. Now run along and have fun. I'll see you both tomorrow."

"Tomorrow? I'm not coming back tonight?" I asked.

Gabriella scoffed incredulously. "Are you crazy? You can't go all the way to—" Ryley cleared his throat to interrupt her and shook his head, making her pause. "Oops, sorry, it's a surprise," she remarked sheepishly. "I can't tell you why."

She came around the bar and hugged Ryley before doing the same to me and whispering in my ear, "I hope you have a good time. He'll be good to you, I promise."

After she disappeared down the hall, I turned to Ryley and smiled. "Okay, let's go."

When we got into Ryley's car and headed down the road, he still hadn't told me anything about where we were going. Judging by the drinks and snacks in the car, I'd say we were going kind of far. "So how far away is it?" I asked.

"Can you not just sit back and relax?" he countered with a smile. "That's why I wanted to pick you up early, so we could get where we're going at a decent time."

"You know, if you piss me off and I tie you to a bed I'm not going to be able to have anyone come rescue you quickly."

He chuckled. "I'm not worried about that. There's going to be no tying anyone up this weekend. I think I got a fair warning after witnessing my brother's demise."

"Does he know you're with me?"

His smile faded slightly. "No, he doesn't. I haven't seen or talked to him since I left Malibu."

"Are you going to tell him?"

"Do you want me to?" he countered.

"Actually, you might not want to," I confessed. "I don't want to cause problems between you two." I'd seen the way he reacted when Ryley texted me; there were some major jealousy issues.

Ryley chuckled incredulously. "Trust me, you're not going to cause problems. Knowing Camden, and forgive me for saying this, but he's probably already banging another chick by now."

That wouldn't surprise me, however …

"Yeah, but he got really angry when he found out you were texting me last night. I know he's not going to get pissed about me per se, but he might get angry about the situation. I left him tied up to a bed, and now I'm out with you. Has he not ever gotten jealous about people choosing you over him?"

Ryley sighed, his gaze guarded. "He mentioned something about it last night. It's the first time I've ever heard him say anything like that before. I know it's not an excuse, but he was seriously pissed off. He tends to say things without thinking sometimes. I wouldn't worry about it, though. I know I'm not."

"Okay," I murmured. "I was just giving you a heads up. Even though he needs a serious ass kicking, I would hate to see you two torn apart by jealousy."

"We're tight, Ash. That'll never happen."

I nodded and was about to change the subject when the radio signaled an incoming call from Ryley's phone. He looked at the number, his smile disappearing when he pressed the button on his steering wheel to answer it.

"Megan, what's up?"

I wonder who Megan is.

Instead of a female's voice like I was expecting, it was a guy's. "Ryley, it's Brent, Megan's brother."

"Hey, what's going on?" Ryley asked skeptically. "Is everything okay?"

Brent sighed and started to talk, but choked up for a second. "Yeah … everything will be fine now. Megan's in the hospital, but she'll be all right. She just has a few bruises."

Ryley tightly gripped the steering wheel, his muscles tense. "What happened? Her ex didn't come after her, did he?"

"Yes, unfortunately he did. She said he wanted her back, but when she told him no he wouldn't accept her answer. Luckily, thanks to you and teaching her those self-defense moves, she was able to get away. I just wanted to call and tell you thank you for helping her. If she hadn't fought back, I don't even want to imagine what would've happened to her. I'm sure she'll call you when she's feeling better."

"Do you need me to come out there?"

"No, that's okay. Our family is here with her. She's pressing charges against him and getting a restraining order. I would've given anything to have been there so I could kick his ass for her. I'm afraid I would've killed him."

"Same here," Ryley growled. "Tell Megan she can call me at any time, okay?"

"Will do, Ryley. Again, thank you for all that you've done, and keep teaching those self-defense classes. Who knows, you might be saving another life."

When Brent hung up, Ryley kept his gaze on the road, but I could tell he was troubled and concerned. "Do we need to go back?" I asked softly. "I don't mind at all. I can come with you."

Wearily, he shook his head and glanced over at me. "No, but thank you. I'll see Megan next week."

"Who is she?"

Ryley chuckled, but there was no humor in it. "It's funny you should mention that. Did Gabriella tell you that she got me out of jail a couple of weeks ago?"

I gasped. "That was you? I knew she got someone out, but I didn't know it was you. What did you do?"

"Well, I was at Cloud Nine and Megan bought me a drink. Needless to say, you can only imagine where things were leading after that. Anyway, her boyfriend caught us in one of the VIP rooms and hit her before starting a fight with me."

Hand over my mouth, I gaped at him, wide-eyed. "He hit her?"

"Yeah, and then I hit him … a lot. I was taken to the station after that, but Megan told them what had happened and swore that it wasn't my fault. She ended up telling me about how he would hit her and shit, so I offered to teach her self-defense classes. When she broke up with him, I was afraid he would come after her, and it looks like he did."

"I can't imagine ever going through something like

that," I murmured. "I guess everyone should learn how to defend themselves. When do you teach the classes?"

"Why? Do you want me to teach you?" he asked, a slow smile spreading across his face. "If you do, you can come by the gym on either Tuesday or Thursday … or both."

"I might have to do that. Maybe I could kick your brother's ass for practice," I teased.

That made him laugh and it was good to see the smile come back into his crystal blue gaze. "I think I'd like that, but I also think it might be best for you two to stay away from each other. You can practice with me all you want."

"Deal."

As much as I tried to stay awake in the car, I dozed off one minute … and the next it was as if we teleported to the Sierra Nevada Mountains. I'd slept for three hours and hadn't even woken up once.

Ryley chuckled when I jerked awake; in a stupor, and not knowing where I was. "Sweet dreams, angel?"

Rubbing my eyes, I sat up in the seat. "Actually, I don't remember if I had any dreams. Where are we?" I asked, staring at the enormous log cabin.

We were secluded, completely surrounded by trees, with no other cabins in sight. The mountains were my home, where I grew up, but my passion was with the ocean. That was why I studied Marine Biology. Nothing, however, could take the place of my memories in the woods with my father.

We hiked, fished, and even camped out almost every weekend when I was a child. I missed those times, but as I got older other things became more important to me. Now I wished I could take those times back.

Ryley opened his door with a wide grin on his face and I followed. "This is my place," he said. "I haven't been out here in months."

"It's very beautiful. Why don't you come out here more often?" I asked. "I'm sure the women love it."

He shrugged. "I wouldn't know. I've never brought a female out here before."

"Well, what made you decide to bring me?"

With a sheepish grin on his face, he cleared his throat and strolled to the back of his car, opening the lift gate so he could fetch our bags. "I don't know. I might have talked to someone about you and asked some questions."

Like Gabriella. She knew I liked the mountains; knew I missed my home and my family. It had to be her.

"Like what kinds of questions?"

He shut the lift gate and started up the walkway toward the front door, but I stepped in front of him with a grin on my face. "You talked to Gabriella, didn't you?"

"Okay, fine, I talked to her and she might have said that you missed home. She didn't tell me to bring you here, though. That was all me. So I admit she deserves a little credit, but not all of it."

Satisfied, I stepped out of his way and let him unlock the door, only to have my jaw drop at the sight before me. The first thing I saw were the snow capped mountains in the distance through the living room windows; the magnificent view was breathtaking.

The cabin had a rustic feel, very masculine, with a couple of deer heads mounted on the walls. However, there was nothing rustic about the spacious kitchen with all of its brand new stainless steel appliances. I loved it, and I could almost imagine I was at home.

From behind, Ryley put his hands on my waist and leaned down to whisper in my ear, "Does it remind you of home?"

"Yes," I breathed. "You have no idea how much I miss it … and my family. They run a hotel out in Aspen. I still remember the day I told them I wanted to go away to college, to study by the coast. They were heartbroken that I didn't want to major in business and take over the hotel."

"When was the last time you saw them?" he asked, holding me close.

Swallowing hard, I bit my lip to keep the tears at bay. "It's been about six months now."

"Why so long?"

"Because," I murmured, turning around to face him. A tear about slid down my cheek, but he caught it just in time and wiped it away. "For the past two years, I've double majored and haven't really had the time go home. I didn't want to tell them just yet, but not only have I been studying Marine Biology, but I've also been majoring in Business Management. I was going to surprise them when I graduated in a few months."

"What exactly does that mean? Will you be moving back to Aspen?"

"Not necessarily. I want to do both, Ryley. I want to work here in California and do what I love, but I also want to be there for my family. During the prime time in Aspen,

I figured I would stay out there and help run the hotel. Afterwards, I would come back here. It would be the best of both worlds."

He brushed the hair away from my face and slid his fingers down my cheek. "I think that sounds amazing. It looks like you have your life all planned out."

"What about you?" I asked. "What's in store for Ryley 'The Rampage' Jameson?"

Grinning, he wrapped his arms around my waist and pulled me in tight to his body. "I'm not really the kind of guy who thinks about the future like that. I live in the now, and right now I need you to change into something you don't mind getting dirty."

"Okay," I drawled out curiously. "What are we going to do?"

Smirking, he tapped me on the nose and let me go, turning on his heel and heading straight for the door. "You'll see. Now go get changed and meet me outside. If you go upstairs, my room is the first one on the right, or if you want, you can pick one of the other rooms. It's up to you."

He winked at me before disappearing out the door and shutting it behind him. My bag was on the floor with his, so I picked them both up and carried them upstairs. When I entered his bedroom, I was glad that it wasn't anything like Camden's at the Malibu house. Instead of the room being all dark in navy blues, it was brighter yet masculine in earthy green tones, more natural.

Setting our bags down, I opened mine up and took out a pair of black yoga pants and a dark green T-shirt with my old tennis shoes. Before I could lace them up, a rumbling came from outside and my heart jumped. I rushed to the window and peered out, only to squeal in excitement. Ryley had two four wheelers parked and ready to go.

I had one growing up in Aspen, along with a snowmobile, but I hadn't ridden in ages. Riding was one of my favorite things to do. Excited, I dashed down the stairs and out the door, only to run right into Ryley as he was coming up the steps.

"Whoa, slow down. I didn't think you were going to be that enthusiastic."

"Are you kidding me?" I squealed. "I love to ride. Let's go!"

Chuckling behind me, he hurried with me to the four wheelers and handed me a helmet. Once I had it strapped on, I climbed up on one of the beastly machines and started it up, loving the feel of that power beneath me. After Ryley put his helmet on, he hollered over at me, "I have to say I'm a little disappointed."

"Why?" I shouted back.

"I was hoping you wouldn't know how to ride so you'd have to hold onto me. No worries though, I think it'll be sexy as hell watching you out there on your own."

Rolling my eyes, I shook my head and laughed. "Lead the way then."

I followed him around the house and through the woods until we got to a muddy trail that twisted, turned, and went up and down the hilly terrain. The mud splashed up and covered me from head to toe, but it was fun. Once we reached a small valley where the trees opened up to a beautiful lake, Ryley stopped and took off his helmet, grinning at my mud-caked clothes.

"Why'd we stop?" I asked.

He patted the seat. "It's time for you to ride with me.

The next place we need to pass through is really steep and I don't want you getting hurt."

"Seriously," I scolded with a smirk, "I can do it myself."

"Just humor me and get on, angel. Do I need to just give you the truth and tell you that I want you to hold onto me?"

"Is it … the truth?"

"Yes, now come on. I told you before I don't like liars, and that includes myself. Get your ass behind me."

He held out his hand, waiting on me to join him. Parking my four wheeler, I put my helmet back on and got behind him. I wrapped my arms around his waist and squeezed, giggling a little.

"Is this better?" I asked humorously.

"Much! Now hold on tight."

He took off fast and headed straight for the trail on the other side of the lake, which happened to go up a steep incline. To be honest, I didn't know if I would make it up the whole way on my own or not. Thankfully, he got us up with ease and kept going on the trail until we couldn't go any further; the trail had narrowed.

"Come on, angel, we're going for a hike," he said, turning off the ignition.

I slid off the four wheeler and took off my helmet while he did the same, smiling slyly at me. Gabriella must've told him *everything.* I couldn't blame the guy for trying, though; it was more than what his brother did, even if it was just for the weekend.

"Please tell me Gabriella didn't tell you every single thing about me," I inquired nervously.

Ryley chuckled and took my hand. "Not exactly, but

just so you know, I like to hike, too. I'm the one who made these trails out here."

"Who owns this land?" I asked. "It has to be over a hundred acres."

"This land has been in my family for years, but I bought about thirty acres of it from my grandparents. They would've given it to me if I asked, but I didn't want to just take it."

"Does Camden ever come up here?"

He released a short, sarcastic burst of laughter. "My brother could care less about this land. He prefers the city life, the beach, and all that comes with it. Other than women, we don't share any of the same tastes."

"How does that work?" I asked, climbing up one of the boulders. The muddy trail turned into giant rocks leading up to the top of the mountain, so I started to climb with Ryley behind me.

"How does what work?"

I glanced back at him over my shoulder. "You know … with your brother. How does it work when you both have sex with the same girl at the same time?"

"Ashleigh, come on, you don't really want to know the answer to that, do you?"

"Hey, I'm curious, what can I say? I was going to consider it at one point, and since I'm not going to ever know I want to hear about it."

Sighing, he said, "First, let's get to the top and I'll tell you all about it."

There were only a couple of rocks left to climb, and when I finally made it to the top I gasped in awe. We were on one of the smaller mountains, more like a hill compared to those around us, but it still had an amazingly breathtaking view.

Taking my hand, Ryley led me to a dip in one of the boulders that was wide enough for us both to sit in. "Are you sure you want to know all of this?" he asked. "It's not exactly a conversation I'd think a woman would want to hear on a date."

"Ryley, I'm an exception to that rule. You and I aren't exclusive and we're not trying to be. Now if I was someone you actually cared about, I could see where there would be a problem."

"How do you know I don't care about you in that way?"

"Because it's you we're talking about, Ryley. You can have anyone you desire, and the last thing you're going to want is to get involved with me. Women follow you around everywhere, and as much as I think you're a great guy, I don't think I could handle it."

"Do you not think I'm capable of treating you well? To stay faithful?" he asked.

I burst out laughing, but my smile quickly faded when I looked over at him and saw his serious blue gaze. "You're kidding, right?" When he shook his head, I sighed and shrugged my shoulders. "I don't know, Ryley. From what I know about you and your past with women, I'd have to say trust would be a main issue. You can't have a relationship without it."

"So you don't trust me." It came out more as a statement than a question.

Regretfully, I blew out a sigh and said, "No, I don't … at least, not with my heart."

Jaw tensing, he turned his head away from me. "Ouch, angel, that hurt."

Lifting my hand to his face, I took his chin and turned him back toward me so he could see the honesty in my gaze. "Things can change, Ryley. I have no doubt that you'll find someone who'll trust you."

"I don't know if I deserve any of that," he admitted regretfully. "I've done too much bad shit and fucked with too many people in this world to get anything good out of it."

He sounded so serious it broke my heart. "That's not true. Look at what you've done for Megan by teaching her self-defense. She could've been raped or beaten to death by her ex if it wasn't for you. You're on your way, Ryley. Not to mention you're doing a pretty damn good job at working me over tonight."

"How so?" he asked, moving closer and putting his hand on my knee.

"You're showing me a side of you I never thought you had. I kind of like it."

A small smile splayed across his face and he moved even closer, his lips only a breath away. "And I have to admit, I really like this part of you, too. I've never met anyone that I could actually be myself around."

"It's a good feeling," I murmured breathlessly, waiting on the kiss I knew was inevitable.

Gently, he brought his hands up to my face and stared at me with those crystal blue eyes of his before touching his lips to mine. "Yes, it is a good feeling," he murmured, slightly pulling away, "and I'm afraid to let it go for fear that I won't find it again."

"You don't have to, Ryley. This weekend I'm yours and I'm not going anywhere. You yourself said that you live in the now. Well, for the first time in my life I'll do the same. In this moment, you belong to me and I belong to you. It's only us ... even if it is for one night."

No one else exists ...

He kissed me again.

CHAPTER 18

Ashleigh

ON THE WAY back to the cabin, Ryley didn't stop when we passed my parked four wheeler. Instead, he kept going, rubbing his hand up and down my leg and pulling me in tighter to his body when it started to rain. Shaking my head, I smiled and held on while he raced us through the muddy trails and back to his cabin.

Thankfully, we made it to his place before we got stuck in the mud and had to hike our way back. "Just in time," Ryley chuckled, taking off his helmet. We rushed up to the front door and underneath the porch to get out of the chilly, pouring rain. Dripping wet, I looked down at my muddy clothes and over at Ryley's.

"You know we'll make a mess if we walk through your cabin like this," I warned him.

He looked me over with a smirk on his face. "You're right, but I think I know of a way to remedy that."

Biting his lip, he lifted his shirt and threw it on the ground, along with slipping off his shoes. I knew there wasn't anyone around, so I slid my shirt over my head and did the same. Ryley then lowered his shorts and boxers, staring at me with heated eyes, waiting to see if I'd reciprocate.

Our kiss at the top of the mountain was only the beginning, and I knew once we got back it would lead to more. My heart pounded and my clit tightened in anticipation, ready to feel what it would be like to be the object of a fighter's desire.

His cock got harder each second he stood there watching me, and even more so when I removed the rest of my clothing. "Now what do you want to do?" I murmured heatedly.

He grinned and pulled me into his arms, his body warm and slick beneath my touch. "I think you know what I want to do, angel. I want to feel your body beneath me, trembling as I fuck you, making you come over and over." Trailing his fingers down over my breasts, he stopped when he reached the spot between my legs and cupped me gently, circling a finger over my clit. "I want to touch you, and taste every inch of your body until you scream my out name, begging me to stop ... but, angel, I'm not going to stop. When you go back to your life, I'm going to make sure you feel that ache between your legs and know it was me who thoroughly fucked you. Not my brother, not anyone else ... me."

Wrapping my hands around his cock, I began to massage him. Instantly, he bit his lip and closed his eyes, sighing. "Good," I said. "Then you can start right now."

Ryley groaned deep in his chest and lifted me in his arms, carrying me to the back of the house. "Have you ever had sex in the rain?"

Kissing his neck, I bit the flesh behind his ear and shook my head. "No, but there's always a first time for everything. However, I'm a little concerned about getting splinters in my ass from the wood."

Chuckling, he set me down. "Leave it to me. I'll be right back."

When he left to go inside, I stood out in the rain and let it pour down on me. It was cold as it beat down on my heated skin, but it felt amazing. After about two minutes, Ryley came back with a sleeping bag and set it down on the patio.

"It's waterproof and guaranteed to help protect you from splinters," he teased.

Taking my hand, he pulled me to him and lowered us down to the ground. The sleeping bag was cold against my back, but Ryley's warmth immediately made everything burn. His lips instantly found mine, along with his tongue as he tasted and explored every inch of my mouth. I moaned and closed my eyes, but Ryley's low growl made me reopen them.

"Don't close your eyes, angel. I have to know that you're seeing me when I fuck you."

His hungered blue gaze penetrated me deeper than anything I'd ever felt before. It was intense to the point it was almost scary. There was passion in those eyes, lust, angst, and above all … desire. I felt it in his touches, in his kisses, and I reveled in it.

"Okay," I murmured breathlessly. "I'll keep them

open."

Satisfied with my answer, he lowered his head, kissing his way down my neck until he got to my breasts. The moment his lips closed over a taut, sensitive nipple, I immediately cried out in ecstasy, yearning for more.

"You taste so fucking good," he moaned, sucking me as hard as he could.

I knew I would have marks from his lips and teeth, but it didn't matter; it felt too good to care. He then trailed his hands down my stomach, making me shiver, before cupping me in his palm and slipping a finger inside of me. When I arched my back, he chuckled and pushed in another finger.

"Does it feel good? I can feel you tightening all around me."

"It's because I'm going to come if you keep doing that," I breathed as he picked up his pace.

"Then let go for me, angel."

Almost instantly, my insides lit up like fire and I trembled as my release hit me hard and swift. It was difficult to keep my eyes open when my whole body shook with uncontrollable desire, but Ryley wanted me to so I did. His heated gaze made it so much more enjoyable, and mixed with the rain falling down his smooth, tanned skin it was erotic. I wanted more and Ryley knew it.

Spreading my legs with his knee, he positioned and stopped so he could pull back the edge of the sleeping bag. "What are you doing?"

"I'm honoring your wishes," he murmured, opening the packet and sliding a condom down his thick length. "As much as I'd like to know what it felt like to feel you without one, I know it's not what you want."

"Thank you," I replied softly. I hated the feel of condoms, but I knew it was a must … especially with his past.

Slowly, he lowered himself on to me and cupped my face with his hands, gazing down at me as he placed his lips on mine. He teased me by circling his hips, grazing his cock along my opening and entering me with just the tip. I moaned, wanting more, and he immediately complied, going deeper and deeper until he was fully inside of me.

Wrapping my legs around his waist, he held me tight with one arm behind my head while the other he used to freely roam down my body, squeezing my breast and rolling my nipple between his fingers. He groaned and thrust harder, this time replacing his fingers with his lips and sucking greedily.

"I just want to fuck you all night, angel. You feel so damn good wrapped around my cock … so wet."

He caressed his hand down my thigh and gripped it firmly, lifting my leg higher on his waist so he could go deeper. The pleasure and pain of him pushing in further made me scream, but it was muffled by his lips silencing me. I bit him in return, making him growl, and sucked his bottom lip hard while he penetrated me with wild and passionate thrusts.

"I know you're close, baby. I want to feel it," he demanded.

Tightening around him, I let my orgasm build and rocked my hips along with his, knowing my release was just on the surface. By the sound of the deep groan in his chest and the feeling of his cock pulsating and throbbing inside of me, I knew he was close. I wanted to hold off a little while longer to enjoy the torture, the way it felt as the orgasm built … but I couldn't.

"Ryley," I rasped, "fuck me harder."

Doing as I asked, he pushed harder. I immediately gave in to my release, screaming out my pleasure. It was even better when Ryley took my nipple in his mouth and bit down while he finished inside of me.

Trembling from the aftershocks of his release, Ryley lifted up on his elbows and smiled, his body shielding me from the rain. "Now that was fucking hot."

"Yes it was," I agreed.

Carefully, he slid out of me and helped me to my feet, keeping an arm around my waist as we rushed inside out of the rain. There was a thick, wool blanket draped across the brown leather couch so he pulled it off and wrapped it around my body while I stood there shivering. Now that his warmth wasn't surrounding me, I was freezing.

"Do you want to take a hot shower and warm up while I get dinner started? I know you have to be hungry."

I chuckled. "I'm starved, actually, but how do you have food here if you haven't been here in months."

Playfully, he bent down and kissed me before pushing me toward the stairs. "My grandmother takes care of my house while I'm away," he answered warmly. "When I told her I was coming up here, she went to the store for me."

"Well, she sounds like a wonderful lady. My grandmother is the same way. I can't wait to visit her at Christmas."

Smiling, he smacked me on the ass and pointed up the stairs. "It's going to be Christmas before we eat dinner if I don't get the grill started."

"Okay, I'm going," I said, rushing up the stairs. "I'll be down in a few. Don't you want to put some clothes on?"

He winked when I looked down at him. "Nope, I don't see the point since I'm about to go back into the rain. Surely you're not going to have complaints, are you?"

"No, not at all," I chimed. "I've never had a hot, naked guy cook me dinner."

"Well, there you go ... another memory that'll remind you of me."

I was going to have tons of memories of this weekend ... some bad, but most of them good. I had to admit, the day was working out perfectly and it wasn't even over yet. There was still a whole night left.

CHAPTER 19

Ashleigh

RYLEY HELD UP his end of the bargain and cooked dinner completely naked. I chose to get dressed in a little pink cami and jeans, but I was starting to think it wasn't a good idea. Sitting there watching Ryley move around the kitchen with his cock hard and ready between his legs wasn't an easy task.

"Are you sure you can't take a break?" I asked.

He chuckled and pulled the parmesan crusted rolls out of the oven. "Sorry, angel, but reheated salmon isn't going to taste very good. Besides, didn't you say just an hour ago that you were starved?"

My stomach growled in reply.

"And that's what I thought," he remarked slyly.

Ryley fixed me a plate, setting it and a glass of wine

down on the table in front of me. Not only did it smell heavenly, it was also my favorite meal: grilled salmon, a black bean cake, and fried zucchini. "So … can you basically cook anything someone asks you for?" I asked.

After wrapping a towel around his waist, he brought over a plate of food and sat down. "Yeah, pretty much. It's not hard to find recipes and just do it."

"I wish I was like that." I could cook, but I typically stuck to the simple things, like baked chicken. "Well, since you know my favorite meal, what's yours?"

He took a bite of salmon and pursed his lips, thinking. "Hmm … it's not that hard to please me when it comes to food, but I think I'd have to say a filet mignon cooked rare and a loaded baked potato."

"That sounds pretty good to me."

Sitting across from him reminded me of being with Camden; when I'd tried to talk to him, and he told me he had no interest in getting to know me. Ryley noticed me staring and lifted his brows, a smirk on his face.

"Why are you looking at me like that?" he asked.

"Sorry," I replied quickly, taking a bite of my food. "I was just thinking about last night when I tried to talk to your brother. He got really agitated with me when I asked him questions. I guess I thought you were probably going to be the same way."

"What did you try to talk to him about?"

I shrugged. "I started off with asking him what he liked to do for fun, and all he said was surfing."

"Surfing was what he and my dad did together when he was still alive. He doesn't do it as much now. What else did you ask him?"

"I asked him how he got into fighting, and that's

when he kind of lost it with me."

Sighing, Ryley closed his eyes and took a deep breath before looking at me with a weary gaze. "There's a reason for that, angel. My father was our coach, and the one who got us into fighting. Camden took it really hard when he was killed. Our mother was devastated, and instead of dealing with the loss, Camden kind of retreated into himself for a while. It took me kicking his ass a few times for him to start opening up."

I gasped. "Killed? How?" When all he did was look down at his plate in silence, my heart hurt for him. I knew it couldn't be easy to talk about a tragedy. Luckily, I hadn't lost anyone close to me to know what it felt like. "You don't have to talk about it, Ryley. I shouldn't have even asked."

"No, it's okay. I don't mind telling you, it's just not fun reliving it," he admitted sadly. I held my breath, waiting on him to speak, and my eyes burned with unshed tears. His pain was so clearly written on his face and it was the first time I'd seen him so raw ... so vulnerable.

"It was the night of my brother's first fight. I didn't have one that night, so I stayed in the corner with my father, tending to Camden during the round changes. My father had trained us for a long time, getting us into prime shape before he allowed us to compete in the UFC. We were so happy that night after Camden won. He was on air ... well, we all were, actually. Especially my father. Afterwards, we went out to celebrate. On the way home, the accident happened."

He paused and gulped down the rest of his beer. "My father was on his motorcycle while Camden and I were behind him in my car. Coming down the opposite side of the road was a car full of teenagers and the driver was texting. He swerved into our lane and hit my father head on."

Horrified, I closed my eyes and put a hand over my mouth to hold in my gasp. "Oh my God," I cried, tears falling down my cheeks. "I can't imagine ..."

"You don't want to imagine it, angel. It was unlike anything I'd ever seen before, almost like being in a bad dream that you can't escape from. After it happened I was so fucking terrified and angry I couldn't see straight. I wanted to help my father, but it was too late. I wanted to kill the bastard driving the car who hit him, but I was too late there, too. Camden dragged him out of the car and started beating him to the point I thought he would kill him. Instead of stopping Camden, I went to my father."

"Was he still alive?"

"Yes," he replied softly, "but only barely. There was so much blood on the road, I couldn't understand how he was still alive. He did have enough time to tell me goodbye and that he was so proud of us. I was thankful I got to tell him I loved him before he passed. Camden, on the other hand, has lived with the regret ever since it happened. Instead of going after the driver in a fit of rage, he wishes he would've gone to our father."

"Is that why he's so closed off?" I asked.

Ryley shrugged, unsure. "I think so. He doesn't really talk to me about it, nor does he ever want to spend time with our family. I think they remind him too much of our father. For the past two years we've won our fights, had our parties, and had our women. It's all that keeps him going."

After wiping away my tears, I sat there in silence while I ate the rest of my food. Ryley, on the other hand, picked at his plate and kept his head down; all I wanted to do was wrap my arms around him and tell him it would be okay. Wounds like that cut too deep to ever be healed. I prayed I never had to deal with that kind of loss, but I knew it would be inevitable.

"You know, I probably need to pick up the four wheeler we left out in the woods. I can't leave it out there until I come back because I honestly don't know when that'll be."

"Oh, I'll go with you," I blurted out, relieved that he was talking again.

His lip tilted up in a small smile, but disappeared just as quickly. "No, you stay here, angel. If you want you can clean the dishes for me while I'm gone. Besides, you've already taken your shower. I don't want you having to get muddy all over again."

"I can always take another one," I claimed.

"Please, Ashleigh," he murmured. "Just stay here."

Getting up from the table, he spooned the rest of his food into the trash can and placed his plate in the sink before disappearing upstairs. The food was delicious, but I did as he said and started on the dishes, placing some in the dishwasher and the really dirty ones in the soapy water. About ten minutes later, Ryley came back into the kitchen—this time dressed in a pair of old jeans and a black T-shirt—and kissed me softly on the lips.

"I'll be back soon, okay?"

Squeezing me around the waist, he exited out the back door and was gone, but I watched him through the window as he left in an off road Jeep he had secured in the attached garage out back.

I wished he would've let me go with him, but I knew

he needed that time alone. I should've realized from the beginning that he was trying to be nice and not say that he didn't want me to go with him.

Not knowing how much time I had, I strolled up the steps to Ryley's room, fetched my phone, and lounged out on his bed. There was a text from Gabriella saying she hoped I was having fun while the other one from Colin saying he needed to talk to me when I had a chance. I wanted to call him back, but being at Ryley's place wasn't the best time to do that.

Instead, I flipped through my ebooks and found a spicy, romantic suspense novel that I'd been dying to read. I'd only gotten through twenty or so pages of it by the time the door opened and slammed shut downstairs.

I wanted to rush down and make sure he was all right, but I stayed where I was and waited for him to come to me. Slowly, his footsteps pounded on the hardwood stairs, so I put my phone on the nightstand and sat up, waiting on him to get to his room.

"Ryley, are you okay?" I asked gently.

His steps faltered, and for a moment I held my breath, wondering what he was doing out there. It just so happened that I got the shock of my life when someone other Ryley waltzed into the bedroom with a surprised yet smug look on his face.

"Well, hello there, sweetheart. I wasn't expecting to see you here."

"Oh, what the hell," I gasped.

Camden ...

CHAPTER 20

Ashleigh

I JUMPED OFF the bed and rushed over to the far side of the room. "What are you doing here?"

Dressed in a pair of dark denim jeans and a tight green T-shirt, he leered at me and moved closer. "You know, I was going to ask you the same thing. Since Ryley's been ignoring my calls I figured I'd try to find him. After he left me in Malibu he said he was going to straight to you. I figured you had him tied up in bed somewhere and left him."

After everything Ryley had told me about their father, I actually felt bad for leaving him the way I did. Yeah, he was a dick, and no, I shouldn't give him any excuses for being that way, but I still couldn't help but feel sad for him and Ryley.

"Camden, I'm sorry for doing that to you. I shouldn't have done it. If I could take it back, I would," I claimed wholeheartedly.

Narrowing his gaze, he moved another step closer. "You just don't get it," he sneered. "You humiliated me by tying me to a fucking bed, and you left me there for my *brother* to get me out. No apology is going to make up for that."

Oh yeah, he's still pissed.

Exasperated, I lifted my hands in the air in defeat. "Then I don't know what else to tell you. All I can say is I'm sorry. I don't know what else to do."

His angry gaze turned mischievous as he looked up and down my body, biting his lip. "I'm sure I can think of something. I must say, you look pretty cute in that little pink top. You definitely look hotter in that than in the dress you wore for me last night."

"Thanks, I guess."

With nowhere to go, I backed into the wall and he cornered me, placing his hands against the wall on both sides of me so I was caged in. "Where's Ryley?" he asked.

"He went to get the four wheeler that we left in the woods."

"You went out on the four wheeler? I didn't peg you as the type of girl to do that kind of stuff."

"That's because you don't know a thing about me, Camden. You made it perfectly clear that you had no interest in me whatsoever," I snapped.

He chuckled. "And you think my brother does? He could give a rat's ass about you. This is all just a game to him. If you think I'm bad, he's much worse. You should've stayed with me; at least that way you knew what you were getting."

About that time, Ryley burst into the room, his voice a menacing growl. "That's enough, Cam! What are you doing here?"

Camden licked his lips and smiled down at me, not even turning around to look at his brother. "I'm talking to the girl who was supposed to be my date last night. I had no idea you were taking her away so I couldn't find her."

"I didn't know you were trying to find her," Ryley replied.

"Yeah, well, I was looking for you both. Thanks for betraying me by the way. I know where your loyalties lie."

Ryley scoffed, "That has nothing to do with it. What Ashleigh and I do is our business, not yours."

"Ouch," Camden sneered, glancing at Ryley over his shoulder. "Actually, it is my business … she agreed to be with me, too."

"Well, that was before you turned into a dick," I cut in. "I may have agreed to sleep with you both, but that was because I wanted to do something spontaneous for once in my life. Not many women can say they had hot twin guys at once. It was exciting, but it's not anymore."

Trailing his hand down my arm, he skimmed over my breast and pressed his body to mine. "It can still be exciting for you. I'm sure my brother wouldn't mind sharing for the night."

Behind us, Ryley growled deep in his chest, cracking his knuckles. He wasn't going to let that happen.

Shaking my head, I crossed my arms over my chest so I could put space between us. "I don't think so, Camden."

"Why not? You were going to sleep with us both anyway, right? Besides, you owe me for what you did. I know I was a dick to you and I apologize. I shouldn't have been like that."

I might've believed him if he sounded sincere.

"She said no," Ryley hissed. "Leave her alone, brother."

Camden chuckled and grabbed me by the waist, shoving me against the wall. "All she needs is a little convincing. Girls like it when the guy takes control."

After that, he forcefully closed his lips over mine and held my face firmly in his hands, not letting me go. My legs were pinned between his, so I couldn't kick him in the balls; smart move on his part, but bad for mine. It didn't really matter anyway because Ryley grabbed him around the neck.

"What the fuck is your problem?" he yelled, ripping him off of me. "She doesn't want you, get over it!"

Red faced and full of rage, Camden jerked out of Ryley's hold and pushed him off. "Oh, but she wants *you*, right? Let me guess ... I bet you've already fucked her."

Clenching his teeth, Ryley glanced over at me quickly before turning back to his brother. Neither one of us said anything, which only confirmed what Camden assumed. He looked back and forth at both of us, settled on his brother, and scoffed incredulously, "You have got to be kidding me! You're falling for her, aren't you?"

Eyes wide, I stood there frozen and completely dumbfounded. Ryley wasn't falling for me ... was he? Our one weekend together was just what it was: one weekend. He knew it, and so did I.

"Camden, you need to leave ... now!" Ryley shouted. He was poised, his fists balled tight at his sides, ready to fight. If Camden didn't leave, I knew there would be a fight, which I didn't want.

Camden straightened his shirt and rolled his neck, making it crack. "Fine, have it your way. While you're here fucking the same girl, I'm going to go out and have a variety. At least that way I know I won't be bored."

"Trust me," Ryley hissed, his eyes narrowed, "I'm not bored."

Both guys stared each other down, never wavering. Suddenly, my phone rang, breaking the trance. Rushing to my phone, I saw that it was Gabriella before I shut it off as fast as I could; I had a lot to tell her when I got home.

"You know what," Camden spat, relaxing his stance and focusing on me, "you two do whatever you want. Just don't say I didn't warn you. At least with me you'd know what you're getting yourself into. I don't pretend to be something I'm not."

With those final words, he turned on his heel and walked away, his footsteps thundering down the steps before the door slammed shut with his departure. Only after we heard the sound of his car leaving the driveway did Ryley really relax.

"Are you okay?" he asked, taking me in his arms. "What did he say to you?"

"Nothing you don't already know. Are you sure this all stems from the loss of your dad, or are you finally going to admit that he's jealous of you?"

He shrugged. "I don't know, Ashleigh. He's been fucked up for a while. I don't know what to think anymore."

Nodding, I stepped back and looked up into his blue gaze. "I want you to be honest with me about something,"

I said in all seriousness. "And I don't want you to lie for my sake."

He furrowed his brows and nodded once. "Okay, what do you want to know?"

"What Camden said … is it true? Are you actually worse than him?"

Ryley sighed and took my hands in his, pulling me back to him. "At first I was," he admitted. "I'm the one who brought the women to him to help him cope. I'm the one who led him down that path. I confess I'm not the nicest guy and I sure as hell have never given a damn about anyone, but I can honestly say that how I've been with you right here and now is who I really am."

"So after you take me home tomorrow you'll go right back to the way you were?"

He kissed my palms and smiled. "I don't know yet, that all depends on you."

"On me? Why is that?"

"Next weekend I have a fight at the Anaheim Convention Center. I want you to come with me."

"Are you sure you won't get bored with me?" I teased. "You're used to switching it up."

"True, but I'm not worried about getting bored."

Licking my lips, I lifted up on my toes and kissed him. "Well, then I guess I better make sure you don't."

I kept my gaze on him as I unbuttoned his jeans and let them fall to the floor, along with his boxers. Immediately, his cock started to lengthen, but I dropped to my knees before he could get fully hard. I wanted to suck him while he was soft, but that wasn't going to work with my fighter. He was ready to go.

Ryley took off his shirt while I held on to his ass and

licked his length, up and down. His hands fisted in my hair as I closed over the tip of him and sucked, rolling my tongue around it, tasting the salty drop that pooled at the top.

"Fuck, that feels good," he groaned. "Don't stop, angel."

Luckily, I didn't want to stop.

I took him in as far as I could and worked my mouth around him, enjoying the way his body trembled. Harder and faster, I tortured him with my tongue until he growled low in his throat and lifted me up by my arms, throwing me down on the bed. He ripped off my shorts and hastily lifted my shirt and bra so he could suck my nipples and plunge inside of me with his fingers.

"You're so wet for me," he murmured huskily. "I fucking love it."

He lifted his fingers to his mouth and sucked them off, keeping his gaze on me the entire time. My clit tightened just watching him.

"Sit back against the headboard, Ryley," I commanded.

Lifting his brows, he bit his lip and smiled. "So I guess this is where you show me how not boring you are?"

I winked. "You know it."

He rolled off of me, sat up against the thick wooden headboard of his bed, and reached over to grab a condom out of his nightstand. Taking it from him, I opened it up and slowly slid it down his cock, loving the way his body responded when I touched him.

As he stared at me with hooded eyes, I climbed in his lap and straddled his legs, only letting the tip of him enter me so I could torture him. Tilting his head, he sucked both of my nipples, one after the other while I circled my hips over the tip of his cock, wanting desperately just to take him inside of me.

"You're killing me, angel."

"Oh I know, but don't you like the buildup ... the tension? How do you think it feels to me only having the tip of you inside of me when I want to feel it all? I want the pain and pleasure of it, to feel you stretching me until it hurt."

Ryley gripped my thighs hard when I lowered down a little bit more until he was fully inside of me. His hands left my thighs to cup my cheeks and hold me to his lips as he kissed me, sucking my tongue when I pushed it into his mouth.

I rode him hard, raking my nails down his back, and enjoyed the rumble of satisfaction in his chest as I milked him. The faster I rocked my hips, the louder his growls became. I knew he was close because I could feel him getting harder inside of me, lengthening.

"I'm going to come, baby, if you keep fucking me like this."

Hearing his strangled moan only made me want to move faster, which made my orgasm swiftly reach the surface. "Oh my God, Ryley," I moaned, arching my back. "I want you to come ... now."

My orgasm exploded all around me, intensifying when Ryley bit down on my nipple and released at the same time, gripping his fingers deep into my thighs. He thrust his hips up during the last tremors of his release, and then settled against the headboard with a satisfied smirk.

"Now that felt amazing," he murmured heatedly.

Slowly, I lifted my hips and rolled over to lie beside

of him; he took off the condom and threw it in the trash bin beside the nightstand. Breathing hard, I put my arm around his waist and my head on his chest while he rubbed my back.

"You never answered the question," he remarked.

"Which one?"

"The one where I asked you to watch me fight next Saturday. I want you to come home with me afterwards."

"So there's no party to go searching for your next conquest?" I asked teasingly.

"Oh, there is, but I won't be going to it if you agree to stay with me. Just give me one more weekend."

Smiling, I looked up at him and lifted my brows. "One more weekend, huh? I guess I can't turn down that offer, can I? At least I'll be saving one girl from getting her heart broken by you."

"Which is all the more reason for you to join me."

"Okay, fine, but only one more weekend and that's it. I have my *own* heart to protect, you know."

His smile faded and his gaze locked in on mine, searching. I knew he could see the truth inside of me, but he wasn't going to make me speak it. My heart hurt too much to speak what was truly there in its depths. For now, I was with him—enjoying my time and he was, too. That was all that mattered.

As I lay back down on his chest, I closed my eyes and let the exhaustion of the day take me under. However, I was able to hear his whispered words as he turned off the lights, and it made my heart hurt even more.

"I have mine to protect, too."

CHAPTER 21

Ashleigh

BY THE TIME I got home Sunday afternoon, Gabriella was bouncing off the walls ... especially when I walked through the door. Her hair was a mess and she was sweaty, wearing black running shorts and a blue tank top.

"Do you not know how to call someone back?" she asked, putting her hands on her hips.

Sheepishly, I shut the door and said, "Well, I was kind of busy. There wasn't really that much time to talk."

Guffawing, she sat down on the couch and patted the seat beside of her. "Yeah, I can imagine. I'm sure being in bed with Ryley all weekend was really time consuming. I wouldn't want to leave it either."

"We did more than that," I scolded. "It was actually kind of fun. We rode his four wheelers, went hiking, and he even cooked me dinner."

"What else?"

"Well … I'm sure you can imagine what else we did."

"Was he everything you thought he would be?" she inquired curiously.

Sighing, I leaned my head against the couch and closed my eyes. "He was more than I could've imagined. It was one of the best weekends I've had in a long time."

"So is that it? Are you two done?"

"No," I replied, tilting my head to the side and opening my eyes. "He wants to be with me next weekend as well."

"Oh my God, you know this is epic, right? He's been my friend for a long time and that's just unheard of. He never goes out with the same girl for a whole weekend, much less two. Surely you told him yes."

"I did."

"Then why do you look so sad?" she wondered, furrowing her brows. "Ryley likes you and he's hot as hell. This will be good for you. What's holding you back?"

When I didn't answer, she leaned against the couch and blew out a nervous breath. "It's Colin, isn't it?"

When I nodded, she bit her lip and sighed. "I thought so. By the way, he came here looking for you late last night. He said you weren't returning his calls."

"Oh no," I groaned, rubbing my hands over my face. "What did you tell him?"

"I told him you weren't back yet from your date. I didn't know what else to tell him. Anyway, he wanted to say good-bye before he left to go to Seattle."

"Seattle? I thought he was only going to go for the

weekend?"

She shrugged, giving me a sad smile. "He said he needed to see his girlfriend, Ash."

Instantly, my heart dropped and my chest tightened, my eyes burning like fire when I closed them. "I see," I whispered. "I didn't want to call him back while I was with Ryley."

Gabriella reached for my hand and squeezed it. "I know you care about him, Ash, and I know he cares about you … but he has a girlfriend. Either tell him how you feel or move on. I'm not saying Ryley is going to be boyfriend material, but at least you could have some fun with him and nothing will be holding you back."

That's true.

"What if I tell Colin how I feel and it ruins our friend-ship?"

"That I don't know, babe. You need to follow your heart on this one. Just give Colin a call, and if he turns you down you have a week to get over it before you go out with Ryley." With a big smile on her face, she nodded and mouthed Ryley's name.

"You want me with him, don't you?"

"I want to see him with a good girl," she stated wholeheartedly. "It doesn't necessarily have to be you, but you're what's good for him. He deserves someone who'll like him for who he is and not what he represents."

"Do you think that about Camden as well?"

She snorted and shook her head. "Camden is a whole other story. It's going to take someone epic to turn him around. I don't know if that woman exists, but I have to believe it's possible."

Gabriella … always the optimist. That was why I

loved her so.

Slapping me on the leg, she hopped off the couch and stretched. "Okay, while you figure out what you're going to do, I'm going to take a shower. Then we're going to order pizza and hang out tonight. Maybe we can spend the week at the beach?" she asked, lifting her brows.

I nodded, removing my phone from my back pocket. "Sounds good to me. While you take your shower I think I'm going to call Colin. I might as well get it over with, right?"

She smiled and backed up toward the hall. "Right. Good luck, Ash. Just be honest with him."

As soon as she disappeared, I dialed his number and waited as it rang ... and rang. *Nothing.* I called him again just in case he couldn't get to it in time, but still there was no answer. Should I text him? Leave a message?

I didn't want to do either of those things, but in a way I wanted the coward's way out and do it without having to worry about hearing him say he didn't feel the same way.

Taking a deep breath, I dialed again, my heart thumping wildly in my chest. When he didn't pick up, I listened to his smooth, deep voice as his recording played over the phone.

Please don't let this be a mistake. The introduction ended and now it was time.

Beep ...

"Hey, Colin, it's me. I'm sorry I didn't answer your calls. Gabriella told me you stopped by and that you were leaving to go to Seattle. I wish I could've seen you before you left. Listen, there's something I wanted to talk to you about. I know in a message isn't exactly the way to do it, but I need to get this out before another day goes by."

Nervously, I took a deep breath and let it out.

"I care about you, Colin ... as in more than a friend. I don't want this to jeopardize our friendship, but if it makes things awkward, I'll understand if you need to keep your distance. I just wanted to let you know before I moved on. I can't be in love with someone that doesn't love me back in that way. If I haven't heard from you by the end of the week, then I'll know your answer. All I want is for you to be happy. If being in Seattle does that for you, so be it. I miss you."

Slowly, I hung up the phone and closed my eyes. Now all I had to do was wait to see if he called me back.

CHAPTER 22

Ashleigh

THE WEEK WENT by and … nothing. Colin hadn't called me back or texted the entire fall break. I guess I had my answer. Thankfully, I spent the week tipsy at the beach, and on Saturday I would be with Ryley with no reservations.

"Aren't you glad you found out now?" Gabriella asked, typing away on her phone. For the past hour she'd been going back and forth with someone, not telling me who.

Turning over on my stomach, I bunched up my T-shirt and lied my head down on it while running my fingers through the sand. It was a beautiful day and I wasn't going to let anything else ruin it.

"Yes, I'm glad I found out. I just wish he would've

called me. Now I'm not going to know what to do when I see him around."

"I know what you can do," a deep voice spoke out. "You can keep your head high and know that you have one hell of a sexy fighter in your corner."

Immediately, I gasped and turned over. "What the hell are you doing here?" Then to Gabriella, I narrowed my gaze and spat, "You told him!"

Ryley sat down on my towel and pulled me into his bare arms. He was in a pair of Hawaiian looking board shorts with aviator sunglasses hiding those bright blue eyes of his. "Now don't go getting pissed. I'm the one who conned her into telling me what was wrong with you."

"And that is my cue to leave," Gabriella replied sheepishly. "I'll see you at home, Ash."

Quickly, she got up, grabbed her bag, and strolled away, leaving me feeling completely stupid and speech-less.

"I can't believe she told you," I groaned. "It's not exactly something I wanted you to know."

"I already knew," he told me. "I've known since the day I saw you two together on campus. Look, the guy's an idiot. Tonight, you and I are hanging out and that's it, and tomorrow we're going to celebrate after I win my fight."

"You're awfully confident, aren't you?"

Ryley's lip tilted up in a smirk. "I have to be. Now get your ass up! Tonight, we're going to have some fun."

"What are we going to do? I thought you couldn't have sex before a fight?"

"Fuck, angel, I can have fun doing other things be-sides sex. I thought maybe we could go out to dinner, and then go back to your place and spend some time together.

I'll even watch an overdramatized chick flick if that'll make you happy."

"Deal," I said, wrapping my arms around his neck. "I hope you know what you're getting into."

"I'm still trying to figure that one out."

So was I.

Ryley stayed the night, and surprisingly enough he held me the entire time ... never making any advances. I honestly didn't think he'd be capable of it, but he did. Instead of him cooking, we went out to eat at a really nice Italian restaurant, and finished up the night watching one of *his* favorite movies ... *Fight Club*. Go figure.

Now we were on our way to Anaheim for his fight against Nick Bradshaw, who was notorious for breaking bones. Ryley was ready, though; I could see it in his eyes as he drove us to the convention center.

"So are you going to have women lined up outside of your room tonight?" I asked.

He looked over at me and smiled. "Probably, but they'll disappear as soon as they see you with me. You're all I want tonight."

I couldn't help but wonder how long that would last. With Colin I knew I could trust him; he was a good guy and I'd known him for years, known everything about him. Dating a fighter who was notorious for womanizing wasn't exactly an easy pill to swallow.

I was scared to fall for him, and I didn't know if my heart would let me. All I could do was stay guarded for a little while longer until I got to know him better. My heart still hurt for Colin, but I knew Ryley could fill that void if I let him in.

We pulled up to the convention center, and as soon as we got out of the car, Camden drove up. He parked right beside us, lowering his window with a leer on his face. "I have to say I'm shocked, brother. I never thought I'd see the day when you stay with the same woman this long. It's a shame really. You'll be missing one hell of a party tonight."

Ryley groaned and took my hand, not rising to the bait. As we started for the door, Camden hollered out behind us, "Save me a seat, sweetheart!"

Not turning around, I flipped him off and kept walking. "What an ass," Ryley mumbled low.

I glanced back at Camden, who took off his glasses and winked. "Surely there are some redeeming qualities in him somewhere … maybe."

Ryley chuckled and opened the door. "Oh, I know there is. I just don't know what it's going to take to find them."

"Have you talked to him since the incident at the cabin?"

"No, but we fight every day in training. It's been kind of fun being able to kick his ass."

I could see in his eyes that he missed his brother; he was lost without him, but trying to go on. "I think you should attempt to talk to him. Work things out. As much as I despise him right now, I know you both need each other."

Ryley nodded, but that was the last of the discussion. During the next two hours, we hung out in his room, waiting for his fight to start. Dressed in his blue and white shorts, with tattoos covering the entire right side of his arm, he was definitely a woman's fantasy come true.

Once his coach entered the room, I left so I could get my seat and watch some of the other fights before it was his turn. I didn't have Gabriella with me, so I sat there by myself, watching one of the Lightweight fights when none other than Camden sat down beside me.

I guess he really meant it when he asked me to save him a seat. His blond hair was disheveled in messy spikes, just like Ryley's, and he was wearing a pair of designer jeans and a thin gray sweater with boots. He was dressed sophisticated, but I knew the truth … he was a wolf in sheep's clothing.

"So you did save me a seat. Thank you, sweetheart."

Rolling my eyes, I snorted and crossed my arms over my chest. "Why are you being this way, Camden? I know you're mad at me, but you don't have to take it out on Ryley. He misses you."

Camden's jaw clenched. "No, he doesn't. He would rather fuck around with you."

"That's not true and you know it. If you'd stop being a dick for two seconds and actually talk to him like a brother, you'd see that things can go back to the way they were. You both need each other. Please, just talk to him, okay?"

About that time, the lights dimmed and then came to life again as the announcer—who happened to be a retired Middleweight UFC fighter—waltzed into the ring and waved at the crowd.

"No fucking way," Camden murmured in awe.

Eyes wide with excitement, he leaned over and said, "This guy's a legend. His name is Forest Jacoby, the best Middleweight fighter of his time. I can't believe he's here."

I guess he's talking to me now.

I glanced back to the ring, at the middle-aged man who still looked in really good shape. His dark hair had signs of gray, but you could tell he kept his body in perfectly good shape by his defined muscles, which were showcased in a tight black T-shirt and jeans.

"Have you ever met him?" I asked.

"No, this is the first time I've seen him at an event."

Forest Jacoby waited until the cheers died down before lifting the microphone to his lips and letting his booming voice speak to the crowd. "Good evening, everyone. For the Middleweight fight of the evening, I've been asked to announce this night's fighters. And since I'm a former Middleweight champion, I've decided to do something special for the winner of this division tonight."

"Oh wow," I breathed excitedly. "This is awesome."

Camden snorted and rolled his eyes. "Yeah, but unfortunately it's on the night I don't fight. Lucky bastards."

I had to admit, his luck did kind of suck.

"Who knows, maybe if Ryley wins he'll be able to get you in, too."

He looked over at me, his gaze hopeful. "You think?"

I shrugged. "Maybe. He does have a way of getting what he wants. I bet if you talk to him he'll be more inclined to include you."

"Fine, I'll talk to him and sort everything out. Happy now?"

"Much."

Forest called out Nick Bradshaw's name and the crowd cheered as he came down the aisle, pumping his fists in the air. He was a big guy, but no more so than Ryley. The only difference was his hair was pitch black and cut in a Mohawk, and his whole body was covered in tattoos; he looked vicious.

In fact, when he gazed down at us, he snarled and flipped Camden off, which only seemed to amuse Camden further.

"I take it you two don't get along," I noted.

Camden grinned and relaxed in his chair, putting his arm around the back of mine. "Nope, not at all. He's mad that I fucked his girl a few weeks ago."

"Well, that explains it," I scoffed.

"Yeah, well I wasn't the only one ... Ryley did, too. It was a good night."

"Great," I mumbled.

Before he could continue, I held up my hand, stopping him. "I don't want to know, Camden. Keep the details to yourself, please."

"Suit yourself, but I'm warning you he's not going to change. Guys like us don't stick to one woman; it's not in our blood. The way he is with you is just a phase."

"That may be so, but people can change, Camden. I even believe that one day you will. Besides, me and Ryley aren't exclusive. I like him just the way he is."

"Yeah right, sweetheart," he chuckled incredulously. "Keep telling yourself that."

Rolling my eyes, I turned my body away so I could at least *try* to ignore him. Being with Ryley was amazing, but dealing with his brother wasn't going to be easy. Thankfully, Forest Jacoby finally announced Ryley's name. Once his song played—"I Will Not Bow" by Breaking Benjamin—I sat up in my chair and watched him walk out. His blue hood was draped over his face, but it didn't hide the smirk of his lips as everyone in the crowd cheered for him. The energy made my skin tingle with excitement.

When he got up into the ring, he took off his hood and handed it to his coach. The second he found me, he smiled, but then it disappeared when he saw Camden beside me. "Come on, brother, kick his ass," Camden shouted, clapping his hands.

Ryley lifted a brow and actually smiled at him, which was a good start. "See, I made him smile," he muttered triumphantly.

Ding ... ding ... ding.

The fight had begun and Nick went on the attack first, swinging and punching like a mad man. *I guess this was his way of getting back at Ryley for screwing his girl.* The guy was absolutely nuts and it was only the first ten seconds.

"Oh yeah, he's pissed," Camden muttered. "But Ryley will know how to handle him."

I sure hope so.

Ryley landed a hard jab to Nick's left cheek, but that only pissed Nick off more, causing him to lose focus. Blood spewed across the mat when Ryley landed a devastating blow to Nick's nose, making him fall to the mat. They grappled on the mat for a few minutes before Nick pushed Ryley off and got to his feet.

Ding ... ding ... ding. That round was fast.

"I'll be back," Camden said, getting to his feet.

"Don't hurry back on my account."

He guffawed and rushed over to Ryley's corner where their coach was talking quickly to Ryley, most likely giving him advice on how to proceed. When Camden showed up and joined them, Ryley glanced my way; I nodded to reassure him that I was okay. They talked back and forth, his gaze intent and focused, until the bell rang; it was time to fight again.

This time it was Ryley who was relentless. His blue eyes were fierce and on fire as he landed punch after punch, eventually knocking Nick down to the mat ... out cold; his head bounced off of the floor with a loud thud. It was a swift win and the crowd went crazy; so did I. Luckily, there were no broken bones tonight. Nick 'The Bone Crusher' Bradshaw was knocked out and he wasn't getting up.

I jumped out of my seat and screamed as Ryley's hand was lifted in victory by Forest Jacoby. "Ladies and gentlemen, I give you the winner of tonight's fight ... RYLEY 'THE RAMPAGE' JAAAMMEEESSOOONNN! The prize for this exceptional fighter is a one on one training session with me each week for the rest of the year."

Ryley's eyes went wide and he smiled as Forest shook his hand and whispered something in his ear. After that, Ryley took off around the ring and fist pumped the air in victory.

"Woohooo, Ryley! Way to go!" I shouted.

With a big smile on his face, Camden jumped into the ring and hugged him, along with their coach who looked on in pride. After they were done celebrating, Ryley jumped over the edge and rushed down to me.

"It's time to celebrate, baby. Let's go!"

And I knew exactly what that would entail.

Celebrating meant skinny dipping in the pool. I let Ryley pick what he wanted to do and that was what he chose. Thankfully, Camden was at a party and wouldn't be back for a while. Even then there was no telling how many girls he was going to bring back with him. I'd always been confident in myself and in my relationships, but never have I had to worry about something to that magnitude.

I just don't want to get hurt.

"Are you getting in?" Ryley asked, watching me from the pool. "The water's nice and warm."

With a smile on my face, I let the robe fall to the ground before diving into the steamy, crystal blue water. The water was almost as hot as a sauna and it felt great … even more so when Ryley swam over to me and grabbed me around the waist, pulling me in tight against him from behind.

He nipped my earlobe with his teeth and reached up to grope my breasts. "You know, I was thinking tonight you could stay here with me, and then tomorrow morning we could go back to the cabin. What time do you have class on Monday?"

All I could think about was his hands on my body … not class. "Mmm … ten o'clock, I think. I can't concentrate with you touching me like that."

His hand slid down my stomach to between my legs, and he pushed a gentle finger inside of me. "What? You mean when I'm doing this?" he asked, thrusting inside of me. Chuckling, he kissed along my neck, making me shiver, and guided us to the edge of the pool so I could hold on.

"Yes, when you're doing that," I responded breathlessly.

Slowly, he slid his finger out and turned me around in his arms. Facing him, I wrapped my legs around his waist. All of my fears came crashing down as he stared at me with those powerful blue eyes of his.

I was scared to care about him, scared to fall in love with him. Hell, I was just scared of him in general; he awakened things inside of me I didn't know existed. I didn't know what he saw in my eyes, but his gaze softened and he kissed me, slowly backing me into the wall.

"You're holding back, Ashleigh. I can see it in your eyes. What can I do to make that fear go away?"

"I don't know," I whispered truthfully. "I'm scared."

Taking my face in his hands, he gazed down at me longingly. I knew he was falling for me and there was nothing I could do to stop it. I just wished I wasn't petrified to let him in. Getting hurt left scars, and I had a ton of them; I didn't want anymore.

"Scared of what?" he asked.

"I'm scared of falling in love with you. Falling in love only gets you hurt."

He leaned down, resting his forehead against mine. "I'm scared, too, angel. I don't know the first thing about being with someone, much less love. Let's just take things slow and go from there. If it works, it works … if it doesn't, it doesn't."

"Will we still be friends if it doesn't?"

Ryley chuckled and held my face in his hands. "Who

else am I going to get to ride in the mud with me?" Spreading my legs, he circled his cock in between my thighs and pushed the tip in just a bit, making me gasp. "Now let's go inside so I can show you how slow I can go."

"Or," I responded, biting my lip, "you could show me out here. Are you up for that?"

He pushed his cock inside of me just a little bit more, his eyes guarded. "Are you sure you want it this way, angel?"

It was my next step to letting go of the pain in my heart … to moving on.

"Yes," I murmured, holding him tighter with my legs. "Let's go slow."

Taking it nice and slow was what he did when he gently pushed inside of me and thrust his hips against mine in deep, penetrating strokes. My body was on fire, burning from his touch, his kisses, and from inside of me. All I could do was hold on tight and let him take me away … to a place where heartache didn't exist.

The next morning, I woke up to the incessant vibrating buzz of my phone, which was locked away in my purse. I hadn't looked at it all night; the fighter sleeping soundly in the bed beside me had kept me up most of the night. It was most likely Gabriella anyway.

Rubbing my tired eyes, I put on his robe and slowly

slipped out of bed, tiptoeing to my purse so I could get my phone. I was right in that it was Gabriella, but … she called fifteen times! There were also other numbers as well that I didn't recognize. What the hell? Plus, there were five voicemail messages.

Ryley had a balcony off of his room, so I opened the French-style doors and shut them quietly behind me. If something was really wrong she would've called Ryley, right? Biting my lip, I waited anxiously for Gabriella to answer the phone.

"Hello," she answered groggily. It was kind of early in the morning so it didn't surprise me that she was still in bed.

"Hey, are you okay? You called me like a gazillion times."

"Oh my God," she gasped. "Did you not listen to your messages?"

"No," I hissed low, my heart pounding. "Tell me what's going on."

She sighed and blew out a nervous breath. "Colin's back, Ash. It was him calling you. I thought you would've listened to his messages and come home. When you didn't, he left."

Immediately, my throat tightened and my eyes burned. "What did he want? He pretty much made it clear he didn't want me after ignoring me all week."

"No," Gabriella replied regretfully. "He dropped his phone at the airport and it shattered, so he was going to get a new phone as soon as he got back. He didn't even think about calling to check his voicemail until he showed up at the apartment looking for you. I told him you left him a message and that he needed to listen to it."

"Did he?"

"Yes ... and then he asked where you were."

"And did you tell him?"

"He already knew, Ash. He saw you on TV at the fight. That's why he tried to get to you sooner. He even drove to the arena in hopes he could find you there. I had to stop him from going to Ryley's house."

The more she spoke, the sicker I got to my stomach. "Why would he do that?"

"Because," she murmured sadly, "he broke up with his girlfriend this week. That was why he went to Seattle, Ash. He wanted to end things with her because ... he's in love with you. He didn't want to tell you until he got back. When he listened to your message I had never seen him so torn up in my life. I didn't know what to do."

"Oh my God," I cried, placing my hand over my heart. "I don't even know what to do. What do I tell him?"

"The truth," Gabriella said. "All you have to do is tell the truth. He loves you, Ash. I honestly think Ryley does as well in his own way. You just have to make a decision ... which one do you care about more?"

With tears streaming down my cheeks, I closed my eyes and hung my head. I had to face it ... I loved them both.

I didn't realize Ryley had come outside until I felt his arms wrap around my waist, pulling me to him. "Hey, are you okay?"

"No," I cried, hanging up the phone and slowly turning around in his arms. His gaze was worried, concerned, but as soon as he looked into my eyes he knew. I had to tell him, and in doing that my heart was going to break ... again.

CHAPTER 28

Ryley

"IT'S OVER, ISN'T it?" I asked, watching her wipe away her tears. I knew Colin was coming back, but I thought it was over; I thought she was over him. "What did he say?"

"That wasn't him I was talking to, it was Gabriella. He tried to call me last night when he got back in town."

"Okay, but you never answered my question," I said, trying to keep my calm. I didn't want to care if she left or not ... but dammit to hell I did. I had women lined up left and right who wanted to fuck me, but the one woman I wanted, longed to be with someone else. How the hell did that happen?

"I'm sorry, Ryley," she cried. "I love him. I've always loved him."

"What about me? If he wasn't around do you think

you could ever love me, past and all?"

She chuckled lightly and placed her hands on my face, lifting up on her tiptoes to give me one last kiss. I was going to miss her raspberry scent, the sweetness of her skin on my lips … the way she smiled. She was the only woman I had let get close to me, and now she was leaving. I didn't want her to go, but I knew fighting for her wouldn't be an option. She didn't want me to fight for her.

All I needed to do was pretend it didn't bother me.

"Oh, I know I would, Ryley … because I already do. You're an amazing man, adventurous, fun, and a passionate lover in bed. Believe me, I had an amazing time with you and knowing it's coming to an end hurts. I'm going to miss you."

"Are you going to tell him about me? About what we've done?"

She sighed and nodded. "Yes, I'm going to tell him. Maybe not in detail, but I have nothing to hide. Besides, he was still taken when you and I started. He can't fault me for being with you."

"You know that if you go to him, you won't ever be able to come back, right? This is the last time we'll be together."

"I know," she whispered, and then turned those lips of hers into a smile, "but I'm sure you'll be back to your same old ways in no time."

Smirking, I tapped her on the chin and stepped back. The more distance from her, the better. "You know it, angel. I don't stay down for long, you know that."

"That's true," she murmured sadly. Smiling one last time, she gazed up at me with her emerald colored eyes and squeezed my hand before letting go all too quickly.

"Good-bye, Ryley. I really will miss you."

"Good-bye, Ashleigh."

For a moment, I didn't think she would leave, but then she walked right past me and out of my life. I'd walked away from so many women, but never had one walk away from me like that. I didn't know how long I stood there on my balcony, at least not until the door opened and my brother stepped out.

"Are you going to stay out here all day? I watched Ashleigh get into a cab and leave over two hours ago," Camden explained. "Is she coming back?"

"No," I answered. "She's not. It's over."

Camden whistled and leaned his elbows on the balcony rail beside me. "I take it she's the one who wanted to leave."

"I don't want to talk about it," I snapped.

"All right, we won't talk about it. You know what'll cheer you up, don't you?"

When I glanced over at him, he had the biggest grin on his face. I knew that look because it was the same look I gave him two years ago. He was using my own therapy against me.

"What do you have in mind?" I asked with a smirk.

Camden clapped his hands and rubbed them together with a mischievous leer on his face. "I'm thinking two this time, brother. Oh, and definitely not brunettes. You've been jaded by one too many of them the past couple of weeks."

That was for damn sure. First, it was Megan at the club and getting arrested, on to Ashleigh who left me for someone else. I needed a change of pace, and getting back to my usual self was what I needed.

"Are you down for it?" Camden asked. "That is … if you're not too heartbroken."

I scoffed and put my arm around his shoulders. "Fuck that, cocksucker. I'm the one who breaks hearts, not the other way around. I say we go out and have ourselves a little bit of fun."

Camden smiled. "I thought you'd never ask."

I was back in the game with my brother by my side. I didn't need Ashleigh, and I definitely didn't need a female to change me into a better person. I was fine the way I was … I was Ryley Jameson.

And nothing was going to stand in my way. The Twins of Terror were back.

The End

TYLER'S UNDOING

A GLOVES OFF NOVEL

Coming October 2014

ACKNOWLEDGMENTS

AS ALWAYS, I have to thank my husband for being patient with me when I'm in my writing zone. Sometimes the house is left untouched, and we have to eat out a lot, but it's hard to concentrate on that when the stories keep coming and demand to be put on paper. I love what I do and he knows that.

To my editor, Melissa Ringsted—Thank you for your patience as well, especially when I rewrite blurbs a gazillion times and I have to get you to edit them all. I cringe every time I send you a message and ask if you can read through another one because I had a story change. You know I appreciate it!

To my PA, Kim Walker—As always, I wouldn't know what to do without you. You are more than just a personal assistant … you're my friend. This past year has been amazing having you by my side.

To my publicist, Danielle Sanchez, and to the owner of Inkslinger PR, K.P. Simmon—I am so glad you both welcomed me into the Inkslinger family. I feel honored to be a part of such an amazing group. Thank you for all that you do.

To my readers—None of this would be possible without you. You all are my rockstars!

OTHER BOOKS BY L.P. DOVER

Forever Fae Series

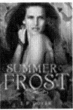

Second Chances Standalones

Standalone (Romantic Suspense)

ABOUT THE AUTHOR

NEW YORK TIMES and USA Today Bestselling author, L.P. Dover, is a southern belle residing in North Carolina along with her husband and two beautiful girls. Before she even began her literary journey she worked in Periodontics enjoying the wonderment of dental surgeries.

Not only does she love to write, but she loves to play tennis, go on mountain hikes, white water rafting, and you can't forget the passion for singing. Her two number one fans expect a concert each and every night before bedtime and those songs usually consist of Christmas carols.

Aside from being a wife and mother, L.P. Dover has written over nine novels including her Forever Fae series, the Second Chances series, and her standalone novel, Love, Lies, and Deception. Her favorite genre to read is romantic suspense and she also loves writing it. However, if she had to choose a setting to live in it would have to be with her faeries in the Land of the Fae.

L.P. Dover is represented by Marisa Corvisiero of Corvisiero Literary Agency.

ALSO CHECK OUT THESE EXTRAORDINARY AUTHORS & BOOKS:

Alivia Anders ~ Illumine
Cambria Hebert ~ Recalled
Angela Orlowski Peart ~ Forged by Greed
Julia Crane ~ Freak of Nature
J.A. Huss ~ Tragic
Cameo Renae ~ Hidden Wings
A.J. Bennett ~ Now or Never
Tabatha Vargo ~ Playing Patience
Beth Balmanno ~ Set in Stone
Ella James ~ Selling Scarlett
Tara West ~ Visions of the Witch
Heidi McLaughlin ~ Forever Your Girl
Melissa Andrea ~ The Edge of Darkness
Komal Kant ~ Falling for Hadie
Melissa Pearl ~ Golden Blood
Alexia Purdy ~ Breathe Me
Sarah M. Ross ~ Inhale, Exhale
Brina Courtney ~ Reveal
Amber Garza ~ Falling to Pieces
Anna Cruise ~ Maverick

STARDUST

I RAN AS quickly as I could, trying my very best to catch up. The large black and red train started to leave the station without me, causing a panic to settle deep into my chest. I ran along the platform, my maroon heels clicking underneath me. My purple and black striped dress clinging to my small frame and my pink fedora hat teasing with the thought of flying off of my head. I had recently cut off all of my hair. In fact, by "recent", I mean, last night. I am a stress cutter and no I don't mean that I harm myself, I mean, that if I get extremely stressed out, I do drastic things to my hair and this was no exception. My hair had been down past the middle of my back, all one length, minus the bits of layering to frame my face. It was naturally chestnut brown, a strong trait in my family, as well as the pale skin, large eyes, and pouty lips. Now...well, my hair is shaggy and bleached blonde. I know, like I said...I am a stress cutter and when I change my look, I do a one-eighty in whatever direction suits me best. It had been four years since I had last morphed myself into something new. I know for some it may seem as if I need to have a therapy session or two, but honestly, cutting my hair had made me feel a million times better after the phone call I had received at eight pm the previous night.

I sped up as the train's whistle blew. The mere sound of it causing my body to tense up. I had arrived late, through no fault of my own. I live in New York City and whenever you plan something, you have to add two extra hours onto it to make sure you have time. Unfortunately it was raining, the city was backed up in traffic and the cab showed up a half hour late. I didn't even complain about it, there was no need. My thoughts were of one thing and one thing only…getting home. I was told to fly, but the train was beckoning me for a very good reason. It was one childhood memory that I always drew upon when living in the city made me feel lonely. Cities can do that to you and I always found it ironic with so many people dwelling in them. You would think it was the last place that loneliness would grip you in the middle of the night, but no. You can be standing in the middle of a packed club and feel as if you are the only person in the world. I never felt like that back home, but it had a lot to do with my dad…and of course, my eccentric family.

The reason I had insisted on taking the train home was very simple. When I was eleven years old, my dad had taken me on an adventure. We had boarded the train with two old suitcases in hand and a need to see all of Pennsylvania. That is where I am originally from. Stillcreek, Pennsylvania and proud of it. My hometown was built on industrial logging, in fact, that was what my dad did. He worked at the mill, he started out on the bottom level, hard labor and long hours. He worked his way up and his last position was that of foreman. He was proud of what he had accomplished and I was proud of him, too.

The train ride was a birthday gift to me. I was adamant about traveling the world. In fact, I had map after map with locations marked on them on my bedroom walls. No one paid attention to it, except my dad. No one being that of my four sisters, Poppy, Violet, Daisy and Rose. I was born last in a chain of flowers, my name being Jasmine. My mother told us, many times over, that she wanted a garden of children as beautiful as the one behind the house. I never thought of myself as beautiful, but she insisted that we all were. I have no idea if it was because I came along after everyone else or if I was just more like a boy, but my sisters were all girly and I was not. I was a tomboy and maybe that is why my dad seemed to bond with me when my sisters clung to my mother.

I remember sitting next to my dad on this train as we watched the scenery go by from our room. The sky was blue, the day was perfect and he said something to me that I will never ever forgot.

"When I die, I want to be taken on a train and you make sure to scatter my ashes from here to the other side of Pennsylvania, Jasmine. I want to be set free. We are all made of stars and to the stars we return."

I remember staring at him as he watched the sky from our window and thinking about how he would never die, he couldn't, he was my dad. To me, he was immortal. I then blinked, pulled out of memory, as I felt a hand take mine and pull me up onto the slowly moving train. I almost dropped my suitcase, a tattered old thing with stickers of different places of the world on it. I sighed and then looked up to see a man standing there, he was dressed in a white button down shirt, a nice coat and jeans. He grinned as I pushed past him and then I hesitated, remembering my manners. I turned back and got caught staring at his shoes.

They were so familiar, like the ones my dad always wore. I looked up and saw his face. His eyes bright and blue, lips a pinkish red. His skin pale, but not sickly in color. He was very attractive. *My* kind of attractive. Young, probably my age, if not a year older. His hair was tussled, that weird style that looks great on some people and completely ridiculous on others. It was dark, a bit shaggy, but framed his face and accentuated his features. His bangs were just a smidgen too long, adding to his "cuteness", that coy *hair in the eyes thing* was happening as the wind blew. It gave him a unique look. One of independence and kind of artsy, my *thing,* when it came to what I found interesting in people.

I grinned, his gallant effort to save me catching me off guard. "Thank you." I said as my hat flew off and away from the back of the train.

We both watched the thing linger for a few seconds before it darted off down the tracks behind us. He jumped. I screamed…I mean, it seemed insane to watch him do it. He landed in between the tracks and ran until he snatched up my hat and then turned to smile at me. His look of triumph soon turned to one of distress as he realized the train was gaining speed. He took off running towards me and I dropped my suitcase and held onto the bar as I extended my hand out as far as I could. He finally reached me and with one leap, his hand was in mine and I pulled as he jumped up. We quickly moved backward and he was against me. The closest any man had been in a while. You see, I was not big on dating, I tend to have strange expectations and it trips me up in the relationship department, but anyway, that discussion is definitely for another time.

We stood there, chest to chest, him breathing hard

and me starting to. I looked up into his eyes and he smelled so good, I could not place the cologne, but it was woodsy and not too overbearing. He grinned down at me, a good five inches taller. He was not broad shouldered, but not too tiny either. I would have to say he was just right. Strange for me to even think it. He lifted my hat and I ignored it as I got caught up in his features. Close up he was even more...

"Here you go," he said as his voice interrupted my inner monologue.

I blinked as I took my hat from him, "Thank you... again."

He stayed where he was and I cleared my throat. Suddenly, his close proximity to me becoming clear. I felt flustered by how much I enjoyed it. I guess my lack of companionship was wearing on me, or perhaps I am just a tad bit off my game. I would have to guess the second was definitely true.

"No problem," he replied as I reached behind me and fumbled with the door handle.

I opened it and backed up, keeping my eyes on him and grinning. I know I seem awkward, I always do and I cannot help it. I stepped through the door and made my way down the hallway. I glanced back as he pulled out a cigarette and lit it. I turned back and made my way along the narrow corridor the best that I could.

He called out to me, "Thank you, for the hand back up onto the train."

I nodded to him and stared for a moment longer than I needed to. I could not help it. He was the cutest thing I had seen in quite some time, not that I was looking...because I don't. Like I said, I am not good at relationships at all.

The train was gaining in speed, so I swayed back and forth, trying my best to not look like an idiot as I made my way down the hallway. I glanced back as the anonymous man watched me, I felt my face heat up, my emotions completely out of control.

I finally saw my door number and slid it open. I peeked in and grinned as I remembered it, just the same as it had been when I was eleven and here with my dad. I slid the door closed behind me and walked to the single bed. I placed my suitcase on it and felt the old dark leather. It was smooth and weathered. Containing memories, as old things tend to do. This was the suitcase I had brought on my trip with him and half the stickers that adorned it were collected by the two of us. We had not traveled to all of these places, in fact, these were simply meant to be a map of all the places we said we *wanted* to go. A wish list, so to speak.

I flipped the lid open and pulled out my dad's picture, it was an old black and white. He was much younger, in fact he was the same age I am now, all of twenty-five. Mom would probably be pissed if she knew I had it, but I snatched it up when I left home for New York and bigger dreams. It was always my favorite one of him. He looked like a writer, pipe in hand, shit-eating grin on his face. As I age I do see him in me, especially my eyes.

I turned and sat down on the bed, holding his picture and then I leaned back. I closed my eyes and felt the sway of the train as the bed felt soft under me. Some people may not be able to sleep like this, but I prefer to have movement and noise. If it is too quiet, I will lay awake all night. My dad was the same way, he used to get up in the middle of the night when I lived at home and eat a cheese sandwich with a glass of milk. I remember walking into the kitchen one night and seeing him sitting at the island in the middle of the room. He took a big bite and then grinned at me as he chewed. I joined him, I think I was thirteen at the time, and it became a strange ritual we had of cheese and milk at midnight. I don't think my mom ever knew that he got up at night when the house was quiet so he could spend some time alone. If I had been older, I would have left him to it, everyone needs their personal space and time respected. I understand that, now that I am an adult, but then? Well, I just felt like it was one more cool thing that we shared that no one else knew about.

I then started to drift off, clutching my dad's picture to my chest. The words "He is gone, Jasmine," echoed in my mind. Dad *was* gone, he had died two days ago while working in the mill. A heart attack they said, sudden…he felt nothing, but how do they know that? How can anyone know what anyone else feels at the time of their death? All I knew is that I hoped he simply closed his eyes and the rest became his greatest adventure, one I would also encounter someday…. one we all have to encounter. That of death.

"Dad," I whispered as one tear rolled down my cheek.

CHAPTER ONE

Cody Baker

SLEEP FINALLY CAME and the dream started out as any other would. I looked up and saw my childhood home, our large, seven room, two story white house. Black shutters flanking rows of windows, with a porch that wrapped around it on two sides. It had two swings, one on either end; in fact, we had two of most things. Two tire swings in the backyard, two treehouses that my dad built and so on. It was a home that was passed down through generations, my mother's side of the family owned it and she grew up there, as did Gram.

It was never an issue for my dad. In fact, his family had come from the other side of the tracks, as they used to say, and my mom was from money. Moderate money, but in a small town *moderate money* was considered well off. We never had to go without, but we were certainly taught the value of things and the hand-me-downs filled my closet. If my sisters wore it, then I got it and, honestly, I loved it. I still thrift to this day and prefer to shop this way. I guess I just like things with character and a history. The only thing I did not enjoy were the dresses, ironically enough I tend to wear them more now than I ever did as a child. I find it funny how we change as we age.

Like I said before, we had two of most of everything. I really did appreciate the second treehouse that my dad had built in the backyard. I used that one and my sisters used the other. It was a private refuge for me. Funny thing was my dad never visited theirs. It had handmade curtains in it made by my mom, a table my dad constructed, small chairs and so on. I think it even had a rug on the wood floor, pictures on the walls, very homey. Mine was practical and built for survival. Before you wonder why, just know that I went through a Zombie Apocalypse stage and that my treehouse became ground zero for me. I had maps on the walls, canned food and so on. My dad loved it and I remember he told me how proud he was of me that I seemed to be able to think ahead, even for "unlikely" scenarios. I did not take that as rude in any way, I was just glad he loved it. He would often visit me there, a place I felt more at home than in the house itself sometimes. My sisters were constantly up for drama, not necessarily bad drama, but drama just the same, and I avoided it. All I wanted was to be ready for the proverbial shit to hit the fan, which by the age of thirteen, I was certain would happen.

My dream continued on as I walked towards the house and then I could hear it. The squeaking of one of the tire swings out back. I walked around the side of the house and saw someone in the swing. As I walked towards them, I realized it was a boy, he had on jeans, a white t-shirt and dark hair. I looked down and felt my palms become sweaty. I wiped them on the sides of my jeans, slowly approaching him with uncertainty. I stepped up behind him, about eight feet out; he stopped swinging and spoke to me.

I listened closely, as his voice sounded so familiar and yet I could not place it.

He stopped moving, his tennis shoes digging into the dirt under the swing as mine had so many times when I was a child.

"Hello, Jazzy," he said in a calm tone.

I started to blink as I heard a knocking...then another and another, until I opened my eyes and the vision of the beautiful boy disintegrated in my mind, but his voice lingered. It merged with the one calling outside of my room. "Room service."

I sat straight up and I realized I had drool coming from my mouth, I wiped it away as I grimaced. Drooling was old for me, I used to do it when I slept at home, but not as an adult. I stood up and swayed as the train rocked a little and then settled down. I stepped up to the door and slid it open and there he stood, my new, attractive friend who had helped me onto the train. I blinked a couple of times and he reached up and took a pencil from the side of my hair. I had just enough left to ball it on the side and I had a habit of shoving pencils into it. It was something I had done my whole life without thinking about it. If you draw on enough maps you end up with pencils and pens in pockets and shoved in your hair. I smiled as he pulled it down in between us and stared at it.

His eyes looked mischievous and I enjoyed it. "Writer?" he asked me. His lip curling up on the edge and only making him cuter.

I shrugged my shoulders. "Part-time poet.... amateur at best."

He grinned. "Mmmm. Interesting, I took you for more of a baker."

I tilted my head and then he extended his hand once again and I found myself shaking his. It was another habit I had. Something my dad always did. Even if he knew someone for over a decade, the handshake was a necessary greeting in his mind.

He glanced down as I shook his hand with some force. His expression told me he was surprised I did it. "I am Cody, Cody Baker."

"I am...." Then I stopped and stared into his eyes with curiosity. "Wait, why a baker?" I asked him and he smiled.

"It's my family's name, I really had no say in it."

I laughed. "No, you said I *looked* like a Baker."

"Oh, you have..." he reached up and touched his cheek as he stared at mine. I reached up and wiped cream from my face and shook my head. I must look insane.

"It's moisturizer. I was in a hurry and I didn't even rub it in, has it been there the whole time?"

He nodded yes and tried not to laugh at me. "You have issues with time, I can appreciate that. I have some myself."

I rubbed the rest of the moisturizer from my cheek as he stared past me and into my room.

"You got a nice, big room here, bigger than mine."

I looked behind me and he stepped in before I could say anything to him about it.

He walked up to the window and stared out, as the gorgeous landscape passed us by. The sky was blue and the leaves were changing. Fall was coming and along with it, my favorite time of the entire year. I honestly could go without summer, spring or winter. But Fall...oh, I loved it more than anything else in the world.

I watched him closely, as I realized how attractive he was. I mean, I had been taken back with him as we stood chest to chest, but I brushed it off as a symptom of the situation and nothing more. He had dark hair, almost black, but with flecks of dark brown in it. I could see them as his bangs fell into his face and the sun from the window danced across them. His jaw was firm, his lips full and he had a light-olive complexion. He looked like the type of man who would have a girlfriend, maybe even a fiancé. I mean, he was too cute to not have someone interested in him. He looked back at me with his blue eyes and I smiled, a little embarrassed that I had been staring at him so hard. He grinned and asked me the logical question.

"So, what is your name?"

"Oh yeah, man. I am sorry, it is Jasmine, but people just call me Jazz for short."

He glanced down at my clothing, of which would probably seem a bit outrageous for some, but I love color and being different.

"Like a jazz club, I like that," he said as he walked past me and to the door. He stopped and turned back to me. "Well, Jazz, I am going to go get a drink and a smoke. Do you want to come with me?"

I shook my head 'no' before I realized it might seem rude.

"Oh, okay," he said as he disappeared through my door and I ran to it and leaned out as the train's movement made me sway on my feet.

"I don't smoke!" I called out to him, he turned around and walked backwards as he grinned at me. He seemed to have no trouble with his balance at all.

"Good thing, it is a nasty habit." He turned and kept

walking away from me.

I bit my lip and then spoke up. If it was the grief guiding me, I didn't care. I felt compelled to not allow him to simply slip away from me. "I could use a drink." I called out to him. He stopped and turned back. I knew from his expression that it made him happy and it felt good, I will not lie.

He looked me over. "I would be happy to buy you one."

"I have money, I can buy my own." I said as I relaxed against my doorframe.

He laughed. "Oh good, because I don't have any money, at all. I was banking on you saying no, you seem to be pretty feisty."

I laughed and narrowed my eyes. I slipped back into my room and ran to my suitcase. I opened it up and pulled out a fresh shirt and jeans. I slid my dress off and slipped the t-shirt over my head. The jeans followed as I ran to the bed and lay down on my back, buttoning them up and tapping my fingers on my stomach. I glanced over at the picture of my dad and smiled at him.

"Did you send him here, Dad?" I asked him as he grinned back at me from the black and white photo. I sat up and walked back over to my open suitcase and grabbed a hot pink scarf with white birds all over it. I wrapped loosely it around my neck. I ran to the bathroom and shook my head, as my hair looked ridiculous. I quickly fingered through it and watched it stick up every which way but the right one. I grabbed some gel and messed with it until it looked presentable and stopped. I stepped back and shook my head, suddenly weirded out by caring so much about how I looked. I shook it and let it get messy again and grinned. This was me now, a bit messy and wild. I hesitated as I stared myself down.

"Why? Just go and have a drink damn it," I whispered. I ran back to the door and slid it open, only to stop dead as Cody stood there, waiting for me. I bumped into his chest and he smiled down at me. I rubbed my nose and laughed.

He looked down into my eyes, his bright with anticipation. "I don't think I have ever been on a date so fast in my life."

I held my hand up to him. "This is not a date."

"Oh, okay. Well, what do we call it then?"

"A chance encounter."

He laughed and I stepped back from him. "What?" as my right eyebrow rose. Another common trait in my family.

He rubbed his neck. "Are you sure you are not a writer?"

I swallowed and placed my hands into my pockets. "Well, maybe a little."

"Novelist?" he asked me and I shook my head.

"No, newspaper. I write articles that no one gives a shit about, in the back…way back, like almost off the end of the paper itself."

He laughed and then parted his lips. I noticed his white teeth and his tongue behind them. I blinked and collected myself. Yeah he was cute, so what? I need a drink. I walked past him and out into the hallway as he followed me. The train rocked and I stumbled. His one hand going to my waist and the other under my arm. He steadied me as I once again felt him close to me. I sighed and he let me go.

I turned to him and nodded. "Thank you, again. I am fine, really, I am. I just have crap balance." He looked me over and I liked it. His expression soothed me. It was odd to meet someone that I immediately felt comfortable with. I had heard about it happening with people, I had just never experienced it for myself.

He smiled, without saying a word. I followed along and then ended up next to him. I glanced over at him and felt grateful. I know it may seem simple, but he was helping me not think about what I needed to do when I got home.

It was not going to be pleasant and I already knew that all of my sisters would be as annoying as ever. Asking me a million questions as to why I was not with anyone, when would I be getting married and be settling down. All things they did with ease. It was not easy to find someone who fit me like that. Marriage was important, it was a commitment to another human being that should be forever. I mean, don't get me wrong. I am not naïve. I know people change and things happen, but finding the puzzle piece that slips easily into your own life is not something I take lightly. I also wasn't even sure who that would be. Would it be a girl or a guy? I had no idea. I was not avoiding it, either. I mean, if I meet a girl and she is the one, then that is how it is and I guess telling my mom and sisters would have to happen then, but without it happening, there was no need to say it. Not yet. My dad was the only person I had ever told that I was bi. Well, him and the one girlfriend I had when I lived at home.

We sat at the table and our drinks vibrated. The bumps beneath the train were causing ripples in the liquid as if something was coming. I looked up at him and his eyes looked even prettier in the light of the bar car. I leaned back and fingered at my drink and he took the initiative to talk to me. I needed him too. I need to just NOT think about my dad and the inevitable fact that I would be attending his funeral. I touched my chest as my heart fluttered and hoped like hell I was not going to have a panic attack. I had had them a few times in my life, normally when the stress of things became too heavy to bear…or, when my sisters would surround me and bombard me with their opinions. I fingered at the small space at the base of my throat and Cody noticed.

"Drink," he said to me and I looked up into his eyes. "It will help," he added, as if he knew.

I narrowed my eyes. "What? I am fine."

He nodded and leaned back in his seat. He glanced out the window and then began to speak in his calm tone. He was just one of those people who seemed to be completely relaxed and in turn, it would relax you too. I sighed and took a drink, thinking maybe he was right. I swallowed as he reached up and brushed his hair back, exposing his whole face.

He cleared his throat. "I had panic attacks up until I was seventeen and then they stopped." His eyes lingered on me as I tried to accept that he noticed. I sipped at my drink and didn't say a word.

He leaned up and interlocked his fingers on the table and I saw his hands, they looked soft, unlike my dad's, which were dry and cracked from years of manual labor.

"You got pale, sweaty. Rubbing at your chest and now you have a red spot. I am not psychic, I just know the signs," he added.

I glanced down and saw the redness on my skin. I adjusted my shirt and covered it up from him as I took the rest of my drink in one large gulp. He leaned back and watched me as if he cared, and maybe he did. Some people are able to care about anyone for any reason. Of course, then again, he could be a sociopath and simply takes on the traits of others and his empathy for plight is heightened. I need to stop over-analyzing it right out of the gate, did I mention I suck at relationships? I do, this is one of the reasons why.

I took one deep breath and stared into his eyes. "Okay, I have them, but not that often," I muttered as the alcohol started to relax me. I figure lying is futile at this point. He obviously notices details.

His eyes remained soft, his tone even, and he sounded like an old friend. To be honest, it was a blessing. I needed comforting and someone to keep me from freaking out. "There is nothing to be embarrassed about, Jazz."

"I am not embarrassed," I said as I looked out the window and he remained calm as he had the whole time.

Then he spoke again as he fingered at his drink. "When I was five, I was in a car accident with my parents and my brother. My parents died, my brother and I lived."

"Oh my God...I am... I am so sorry." I said as he shrugged his shoulder and looked towards the bar. He nodded to the bartender and the man started to make a new drink for him. I looked at the bar, too, and Cody spoke up.

He held two fingers up to the man. "Make it two, please."

The bartender nodded and I sighed, looking at my empty glass as Cody finished off his.

"I just can't imagine going through that, I am so sorry."

"I can't imagine it, either," he said to me and I shook my head slightly and narrowed my eyes as it confused me.

He then looked at the bartender as he brought two new drinks over to us and sat them down on the table. Cody handed him a credit card and told him to keep it on tab. I shook my head 'no' and Cody held up his hand to me.

"Are you always this difficult?" he asked.

I smiled and allowed the bartender to take his card.

"I thought you said you had no money?" He laughed under his breath.

"Credit cards only. It's not real money, just borrowed."

"True," I said as he looked back towards the window and took a drink.

I studied his tight jawline. "So you said you cannot imagine it, what do you mean by that? I mean, a car accident is a horrible thing to live through and…well, how do you not know?"

He kept his eyes on the scenery going by the window.

"I don't remember anything about that day, nothing at all."

I watched him very closely as he took yet another drink and then hissed as it burned his throat going down. I stared at mine and he looked at me.

His eyes narrowed and his grin returned, "Don't."

I leaned back and stared into his eyes, "Don't what?"

He grinned and placed his arm up on the back of his booth in a relaxed manner.

"Pity me, I am totally fine. I can see it on your face, you feel sorry for me and there is no need to. I am just telling you this so you can relax and understand that I am damaged too."

I shook my head 'no'. "I did not pity you in any way. I just, I mean, I think it is probably best that you don't remember it and I am not damaged, I mean, I may be a little bit, but I never meant for you to take it as I thought you are damaged in any way."

He turned his head and moved his hair and I saw the scar on his scalp. It was white and ran about two inches in length. "Look," he said, completely ignoring my sudden defensive position.

"Ouch." I whispered.

He looked back at me and spoke as if it was every day and nothing to be alarmed by. "Yeah, I slammed my head into the side window, busted the glass and was thrown from the car."

I fingered at the base of my neck as the thought of it disturbed me. To think of a child going through that was horrifying. "Oh my God."

He pointed at me. "See, it is that look, right there." He stared at me and laughed.

I stopped messing with my skin and lowered my hand to my lap. "What?"

"The 'Oh my God' tone, I am fine, I am, Jazz. In fact, it was somewhat of a blessing to be shielded from it. I mean, who would want to remember something like that any way?"

I shook my head and decided to explain myself. "Listen, I am just reacting like any normal human being would to something like that. It was a terrible accident; you got hurt and your parents…"

He interrupted me and said what I did not want to. "Died."

I sighed and fingered at my glass on the table, "Yes,

that. The dying thing."

He leaned up. "Who died in your life, Jazz?" I parted my lips and almost said it as his words beckoned me to give into him. To just lay it all out for this attractive stranger right here and now. I felt the train starting to slow. I looked at the bartender who stared out the window.

"Are we stopping?" I asked him.

He dried the glass in his hand and set it down. "No, we slow down as we go over the long Bayberry Bridge. I think they do it for the tourists on the train. Gives everyone a better view of the valley," he said.

Cody leaned towards me from across the table and grinned. "Do you want to see something cool?" he whispered as his left eyebrow rose a little bit. His expression tainting me into saying yes.

I raised an eyebrow and he stood up, extending his hand to me. I took it and he pulled me out of the booth. I looked back at the bartender as he nodded to me.

"Come with me," Cody said as he started to walk, my hand in his and me feeling a bit awkward. I had never had someone I just met take my hand and lead me anywhere, but I guess there is a first for everything. He just seems to be so comfortable in his own skin and a chameleon of sorts. I bet he could adapt to anyone or any situation very easily. I envied that in him, as I would guess most people would. It is true freedom to not be bound to insecurity and the opinions of others around you.

We stepped through one car and then another. Passing my room and then ending up at the end of the train. He pulled out a card and jimmied the door open and the wind blew in, cold and refreshing for a second. He stepped through, his hair blowing up around his face with his hand outstretched towards me. I took a breath and tried to re-member the girl I once was, the tomboy with no fear. I shed my reservations and reached out, taking his hand and stepping out onto the platform. He slid the door closed behind me as he leaned up and I found myself close to his chest once again. The heat coming off of him countered the chill in the air. He backed up and looked me over, his expression telling me that he was happy that I did this with him without question.

"Come on," he said loudly as he pulled me to a ladder and placed me in front of him. I started to climb after I looked back at him and he nodded. I stared up as I climbed, remembering the first time I had climbed my treehouse. It was frightening, but I did it anyway. That time, my dad had been behind me, making me feel safer. This time, Cody was and I know I really have no idea who he is, but sometimes a stranger can be a guardian angel. Someone who can make you instantly feel better no matter what is going on. I kind of felt like that with him and whether it was the grief, the alcohol settling in, or my old ways, I didn't care. It felt good to just let go again.

I reached the top and climbed onto the roof of the train. The wind was daunting and I felt as if I would slide off, but just as fear started to set in, he joined me. I felt his arm around my waist and he turned me and sat behind me. He took the brunt of the wind as I sat in front of him and looked out into the skyline. The sun was starting to set and the brilliant colors of pink and blue lingered behind. The chill in the air seemed to fade as his chest rested against my back. The sun broke one last time through the clouded sky and I closed my eyes as everything lit up in a gold hue.

Cody wrapped his arms around me and for one moment, we sat there, not as two strangers, but as two souls sharing something very special together. There was nothing awkward about it and with that, I leaned back and he held me. I grinned as the sun continued to light both of our faces up and no words were needed, I mean, to be quite honest, they would have just ruined the moment. Sometimes you just have to shut up and listen. Listen to life and the beauty all around you.

CHAPTER TWO

Misunderstanding

"OH CRAP," I muttered as I rolled over and saw him lying in my bed. I pushed my blonde hair out of my bloodshot eyes and stared at him. His hair was fine, he looked peaceful and my head was aching with the five drinks I had downed. The train swayed and so did my stomach as a bottle rolled across the floor and hit the wall. I slid out and saw it. It was wine. So not only had I drank liquor, but I brought him back here with a bottle of wine. Just fabulous, and so not like me. Do not get me wrong, I am certainly NOT a prude, but having sex with complete strangers, whether I liked them or not, was not my style. I knew better. It could be messy and I am not one for messes, I prefer nice and simple, except for my clothing.

I stood up and stumbled as I started to walk towards my small bathroom. I reached for the door and heard his voice. I closed my eyes, sighing, as I had to turn around and face him.

"Good morning," he said.

I grimaced and hesitated for a few seconds. I mustered up the courage to face him. I turned and half smiled. It was awkward, I know that it was. It felt awkward and I felt stupid for allowing this to happen.

I nodded as if I didn't know him at all. "Good morning," the tone of my voice sterile, even to my own ears.

He ignored it and sat up. "Well, I guess I should get up. I am sure they have breakfast ready."

I crossed my arms on my chest and he stood up and looked at me. He started to button his shirt up as I tried to ignore his chest that was all muscular and enticing.

"You go ahead, I am not hungry. I just don't eat this early...not usually."

He continued on as if we were now a couple, or at least it felt that way. "I can go and bring something back for you, Jazz."

"No, really. It's no big deal," I said as my voice sounded colder than I meant for it to. I shook my head 'no' as he sat down and slid one shoe on then the other. I watched him until he stood up and rubbed his hands through his hair. He stepped towards me and I stepped back. He stopped and looked me over.

"You look really good in the morning."

I sighed and then looked down, suddenly realizing that I was in my underwear.

"Oh...my.... God," I said as I looked back up at him.

He smiled and walked to the door. He then stopped and turned back to me. "Thank you," he said softly as I watched him go.

I ran into the bathroom and threw up, as I could not hold it back any longer. I stood up and stared into the mirror. I looked horrid so his comment was pity, the exact pity he had told me to avoid with him. I closed my eyes as I gripped the sides of the small sink.

"Unbelievable," I whispered as I ran the water in the

sink. I reached in and scooped water into my mouth and spit it back out. I started the shower up, letting the hot water steam the small room up until my reflection was gone and I was not forced to look at myself any longer. As if I even know who I am right now.

I SAT IN the breakfast car and sipped my coffee, strong and unrelenting, just as I needed. The bitter taste on my tongue almost felt like I deserved it. I heard the door slide open and glanced behind me to see Cody coming in. He looked as if he had showered too. I guess he just could not come straight down here, but I wished that he had. Not to be rude, but seeing him was not what I really wanted. I adjusted my sunglasses on my face and turned back in my seat, not willing to even invite him over, but when he slid in across from me I was forced to deal with it.

"Did you eat?" he asked me and I shook my head 'no' and took a drink of my coffee. Each sip was getting me closer to feeling normal again. I needed to sober up. I needed to get back to reality and not some romantic encounter with a guy who happened to be on the same train as I was. So ridiculous.

"You know, they say that if you skip breakfast you just set yourself up for failure."

I smiled and raised an eyebrow as I set my cup down and the coffee moved in it with the vibration of the train. I cleared my throat. "I drink coffee in the morning, and then I eat lunch and dinner, I never do breakfast and I rarely deal with failure."

He bit his bottom lip and continued on. "Well you look thin," he said as his plate showed up and it was full of pancakes and eggs. A side of three pieces of bacon took up what little room was left on the plate.

I smelled it and my stomach growled, but I played it off. I really don't do breakfast that often, I guess saying 'never' was a white lie.

"Oh really?" I asked him and he grinned as he took a big bite of his pancakes.

"Well, you are just small, I guess."

I took my sunglasses off and squinted as the light in the car did me no favors. He glanced up at me and snickered. They were bloodshot and dark circles sat under them.

"So are you implying that I have a eating disorder now?"

He stopped chewing and leaned forward. "Do you?" he muttered and I rolled my eyes.

"No, I do not," I said quietly.

"You are so grumpy in the morning, it is kind of cute."

I sighed and put my sunglasses back on, "Listen, last night was…" I picked up my coffee.

He stopped chewing and sat back, wiping his lips with his napkin and then taking a drink of his orange juice. I watched him closely and felt like an ass. It had been the two of us, not one. I had no right to be such a shit about things.

"Last night was great," he said as he watched me.

I bit my bottom lip for a split second and then stood up. He reached out and touched my wrist, but I pulled from him and left the car. I can't do this. I know I should say more and be a bigger person, but I am emotionally compromised right now. I cannot think of any other way to explain why I would even consider doing something like…well, you know, I guess what pisses me off the most is that I cannot even remember it. He is so pretty and if I am going to torture myself with it then I would love to at least know how it felt to be with him.

"Jazz," he called out to me as I left him there. I kept walking even though everything in me wanted to stop and just go back and devour his plate of food. So much for not being "drama" like my mom and sisters. Perhaps I was more like them than I ever knew.

I SAT IN my room and stared out the window as the scenery started to become more familiar. I leaned up and looked out across the hillside. It was beautiful and packed with trees changing colors. It was pulling out of Summer and into Fall. Nothing was as beautiful as the seasons changing in Pennsylvania. Not to me, anyway. I did not leave because I hated it here, I left because I had always dreamed of living in New York and when the opportunity presented itself, I took it. I had gone to college there for writing and, luckily, I landed a job at the New York Times, just working as an assistant on small articles, but still, baby steps. I was grateful and although my dad was excited when I told him on the phone, his pause told me that he missed me and I appreciated being missed by someone. My sisters were too busy with their families and kids. My mom was enjoying being a grandmother and I was just wanting to carve a small space out for myself, and maybe stop being referred to as the 'youngest' or the 'baby'.

The train went on for another hour or so as I listened to my music, my earbuds drowning out any noise. I leaned back and watched the trees, as they became thicker and thicker and knew that I was coming home. I had not been here in a year and bad weather had ruined Christmas. I felt bad for that, I really did. The airports closed with a terrible ice storm and I spent the last Christmas my dad would be alive with a few friends from work. I wanted to come home, but now the weight of missing it was a thousand times worse. I know it is not my fault, but still. If I had known, I would have found a way, but we cannot live in regret. He always told me that and I have to believe it. He knew that I loved him, he knew. In fact, he was the ONLY person in the house that I never had a fight with. That says it all right there.

The train started to slow down and I sighed as I pulled my earbuds out. I knew it would not be easy and I could only hope that my sisters would give me a break, but who am I kidding? I had not been home for a year and now, well, this would not be a happy reunion. Not by a long shot. I stood up and grabbed my suitcase as the train slowed and then stopped at the station I always loved. It was located in the heart of Stillcreek and was really the reason our town had survived when so many others fell to economic ruin. Trust me, there are plenty of people who love the idea of coming to a "small town" and hitting a bed and breakfast. Most of our visitors came from New York, they were nice enough and just wanted to get away from the city. Stillcreek would provide that in abundance with the rows of townhouse-style homes, lush hillsides and abundant forests. It looked like it was taken from a post-card. We lived on the "old side" of town, the area that had the vintage homes. Ours was from the 1800's and I loved it, even on storm-filled, spooky nights it enchanted me. I don't think anything was as fun as scaring the shit out of my sisters and getting them screaming through the house. I can't say that my mom agreed, but Dad always laughed under his breath. I then spotted Poppy and Violet from my window. I think out of all of them, they were the quickest to annoy me. I sighed and gripped my suitcase in one hand as I decided to just suck it up and go. I mean, they have to be softened by what has happened. At least I can hope that they were.

I stepped out of my room and saw the people in the hallway. I moved down the hallway and past a couple kissing as I turned my head. I pushed on and then he stepped out and I once again found myself face to face with Cody's chest. I looked up and half-grinned at him as he smiled back at me.

"This is your stop, right?" he asked me and I nodded to him. He sighed and stared down at me, "I can walk you to the exit."

"Okay, I would like that," I said as I suddenly felt like having him do that would help me actually get off of the train. I stopped when I saw the door and he reached out and opened it up for me, but that was not my intention at all. I didn't expect him to do anything like that. I stood there and gripped my suitcase until my knuckles turned white. I was frozen in place, emotionally and physically. I blinked as I felt him take it from me and step out. He reached his hand up towards me and I took it. I stepped off of the train and was immediately smacked in the face with the familiar smells of Stillcreek. It smells like a bakery here, fresh breads and pastries and my stomach growled as he grinned. I looked past him and spotted Poppy and Violet as they whispered to each other and then started to head my way. They both examined Cody with their eyes, I was mortified, if they found out that I had…it would be a disaster of epic proportions. News traveled faster with them than with the Internet. I stood there as Cody narrowed his eyes and studied my facial expression, which must have told him everything.

"You okay?" he whispered to me. His eyes soft and caring.

I swallowed hard and then they reached us as Cody turned and smiled at the two of them. Poppy reached out and touched my hair as Violet stared at Cody.

"What have you done?"

"I cut my hair, people do that."

"Mmm," she said as she pulled her hand back and looked it over. "It is short and you killed it with the bleach. Did you pick up that conditioner I told you about?" I shook my head 'no' and she went on. "You need it, it looks horrible."

I sighed and Violet extended her hand to Cody.

"I am Jasmine's older sister, Violet, and you are?"

Cody smiled and took her hand, immediately kissing it and she was impressed. She was strange sometimes about things and old school stuff impressed her the most. You would think she was born in the wrong century.

She grinned as Cody let her hand go and continued to smile.

"Cody Baker," he said as Poppy stepped in and looked him over.

"You did not tell us you had a boyfriend, Jasmine."

"I…" I started to say. Cody interrupted me before I could explain anything.

"Well, it was supposed to be a surprise." He glanced

at me and he looked as if he was so enjoying this. "Jazz was going to bring me home before now, but my work keeps me busy." I raised an eyebrow and stared at him, totally shocked as the words just flowed from him, as if they were truth.

"And what work do you do?" Violet asked him without any hesitation.

"I run a company, I mean, it was my father's, it was left to me, investments and business, I am sure it would bore you."

"I never get bored about money," Poppy said as I rolled my eyes and then cleared my throat. They both looked at me and I looked behind them.

"Well, Mama wanted us to meet you here and drive you home."

I spoke before I worried about how they would react. "I want to walk," I said as quickly as they offered. Violet crossed her arms on her chest and Cody placed his arm around me.

"I asked her too, she has told me so much about this town, I just wanted to walk, I hope that is okay. It was my idea." He leaned over and kissed me on the cheek as I stared straight ahead like a deer in headlights. His arm shook me as they both stared on.

Violet nodded and smiled at him. It was amazing how charmed she was by him.

"It is beautiful here. I have lived here my whole life," she said, like me and Poppy were not even there. Poppy pulled on her arm and Violet smiled again as they started to walk away. Poppy looked back and mouthed the word "divorce" to me and I was kind of shocked but Violet's sudden need to get Cody's attention made more sense. I mean, Violet had married her Prom King, star football player, Josh Wieling and I thought she would own his soul from this life to the next. I guess that deal with the devil had fallen through. I relaxed as they rounded the corner and left me standing there with Cody. He looked at me with a calm expression on his face.

"Well?" he asked as he held his arm out and I stood my ground.

"Listen, I appreciate that, but you can get back on the train. I will just tell them you got called to work." He leaned into my face and his lips were just mere inches from my own. He smelled amazing, just as he had the day before.

"Nothing happened," he whispered to me as his eyes stared deeply into mine.

I stepped back as the words broke the trance I was in. "What?"

He stood up straight and looked me over. "Nothing happened. You drank too much, I got the bottle of wine because you asked for it and then you fell asleep."

I swatted at him as he backed up and laughed at me. He held his hands up. "Grumpy and violent. I love it."

I shook my head and walked past him as he watched me. He called out and it stopped me dead in my tracks.

"Have fun with your sisters." I hunched my shoulders as the thought of it really sucked. I mean, it would be hard enough to handle the funeral and all of them together...but this? The promise of a man in my life who would not be there? Ugh.

I sighed and then turned back to him and placed a hand on my hip. I walked towards him and stopped about three feet away.

"It is your fault that they think we are dating."

"I know, I thought I was helping you. I mean, you said all kinds of heinous stuff about them last night when you were drunk and I felt sorry for you. I mean, not like in a pathetic way, I just have an older brother and he is an asshole."

"I did not," I said as he nodded his head 'yes' to me.

"Yes, you told me a lot of things."

I rolled my eyes. "How much older is your brother?" I asked him and he rubbed his neck.

"Four years, and he thinks he knows everything but he doesn't. It annoys me."

I sighed and could just hear it now, it would be a blood bath if I showed up alone. It would give them all a reason to grill me and maybe with Cody there, I could avoid it and just do what I came here to do, bury my dad.

"Nothing happened at all?" I said and he leaned forward.

His eyes lingered on my lips. "Well, you almost kissed me, but I stopped you. I mean, you were drunk."

I felt flustered, my cheeks turning red. "I did not."

"You did so."

I rolled my eyes. "I don't just kiss people."

"Oh I know, you said that before you tried to do it."

I raised an eyebrow and stared him down. "I was drunk."

"And 'emotionally compromised' if I remember you correctly," he added as I sighed. Damn it. He was just too comfortable to be around. I hesitated and then heard the train whistle blow to give everyone a five-minute warning.

He crossed his arms on his chest. "It is me or you go in with no sword."

I bit my lip. He would make things easier and diffi-cult all at the same time. What the hell was I thinking?

The whistle blew again. "Okay, fine." I said as he grinned at me.

He ran off, calling out behind him, "Let me get my bag."

"Fine," I said as he jumped back on the train and I could see him moving through the cars. He reached his room and stepped in, grabbing his backpack, then he looked up and saw me through the window. He stopped for a minute as he looked me over and I turned and stared at the people on the platform. He returned to me and slung his backpack over his shoulder as I watched him. I had to be completely insane or in the middle of a breakdown to be allowing this to happen.

He waved his hand like a wand in front of him. "La-dies first," he said to me as I started to walk with him alongside me.

We rounded the corner and there it was. Stillcreek. I stopped and watched the trees blowing and smelled the air as he looked around too.

"This is nice," he said as his eyes wandered over the old structures and the cobblestone street running down Main. It still looked just like a postcard. The mixture of bread and berries wafted up around us and he smelled it as I did.

I looked at him and nodded. "It is beautiful, it always has been. I guess I just don't think about it in the City, I am busy working." He nodded to me as we continued on, past the downtown shops and everything until we reached my side of town. I had not said anything to him as we walked, but I did notice him studying everything. I stopped on the corner as the light sat on red and he nodded.

"This is something else, Jazz. I mean, it looks like a painting."

I glanced at him. "I loved it here, minus my sisters some days, but it was not all bad."

"Did you leave because of them?" he asked as the light changed and we started to cross the street.

"No, I left because I wanted too. I dreamed of living in New York City and after I graduated from college there, I stayed."

"I don't know, Jazz, if I had come from a place like this I would have found a man, got knocked up and settled down."

"Oh really, so *you* can get knocked up then? Medical breakthroughs astound me."

I stopped walking and then he busted out laughing. "I was kidding, people can do whatever they want to do and who is to say that a family is a bad thing? I wish I could remember being in a family, I do...I mean, I really do." I looked him over.

"Listen, I am sorry. I did not mean to assume that we did anything or that you would take advantage of me. I just was not myself last night. Not at all. I don't just meet people and try to make out with them and then invite them into my bed."

He grinned and looked into my eyes. His blue eyes brighter with the mid-day sun shining in them.

"I felt your boob."

I stepped back from him. "What?"

"Just a little grab, it was nothing special."

"Oh really?" I said as I could feel my temper rising.

He pointed at the palm of his hand. "I mean, it was

small, barely fit in my hand."

I swung my suitcase at him and caught him on the side as he laughed at me.

"Are you serious?" I yelled and he held his hands up.

"About the size or if I did it?"

"Cody!"

"I did NOT grab your boob okay? I am just kidding!"

I shook my head and stepped back from him. "No lie?"

"No lie, Jazz, I did not touch you."

"Not even a little?"

He tilted his head as I sounded as if I wished he had.

"I mean, I am taking you to my house, my family lives there."

"I swear I did not touch you, I was just kidding. I swear, you looked sad, I was just trying to make you laugh."

I narrowed my eyes. One thing my dad always told me was that a person could not stare you in the eye if they were lying and I started to relax as he stood up straight and shook his head.

"I swear," He added as he stepped up and I got caught up in his eyes again.

"You are a dick."

"I can be," he said as he grinned.

I turned and walked away, he stood there until I stopped and called out to him.

"Come on," he grinned and followed me. I stopped and turned to him

"Why?"

He stopped and stared me down. "Why, what?"

"I mean, you didn't even try to kiss me?"

He grinned and shifted from one foot to the other. "Not yet," he said to me and I turned as my heartbeat fluttered in my chest.

CHAPTER THREE

Two Rooms

I RAISED MY hand to knock on the door and Cody reached past me and opened it up, as if he lived here. I have no idea why I was going to knock. I am completely off of my game and feeling foreign, even to myself. I mean, here I am bringing a man home, who I barely know, to try to avoid all the same old shit. I could hear my mom's voice in the other room and it only took about fifteen seconds for the sisters to descend on us like vultures. Violet came in first and was grinning like she could not be any happier to see anyone. It kind of disturbed me, followed by Poppy, Daisy and Rose. I set my suitcase down as they all stared at me and then the attention went straight to Cody, of course. Evidently he was good for diverting their attention from me. I could at least be grateful for that.

"Well, look at you," Daisy said as Rose smiled. Violet and Poppy stood by them and the four of them reminded me of how they would be when I was younger. It was always a wall of them versus me.

"Hi," I said as I waved a hand and they all fawned over him until mom stepped into the room. The chatter suddenly stopped and they parted as she stepped through them. She walked up to me and then gave me a big hug, which was unlike her. I looked towards my sisters and they looked as if it was something I should get used too. She held onto my arms as she stepped back and looked me over.

"You need to eat and what have you done to your hair?"

"I do and I cut it off."

"Mmm," she said, as she looked me over.

"I said the same thing," Cody added as my mom's eyes went to him. She let me go and it was on. I mean, he asked for it. Mom walked up to him and looked him over. Her gaze steady on him. She would always be the same. Strong and intimidating. There wasn't a resident in this town who did not know her or try to avoid her wrath. She wasn't mean, but you just have to know her and how she is. To outsiders, she would appear cold, but the truth was she was not. Just appeared that way.

"So you are dating Jasmine, Cody Baker," she said, it was not even a question, just a statement, like she was known for. I grinned, I had too. If any payback was coming to Cody for messing with me it would be paid in full now.

He nodded and she crossed her arms on her chest, I am sure it reminding him of me. If one thing was true, I got my temper from her and my attitude. My desire for travel came from my dad.

"How long?"

"I'm sorry?" Cody asked her.

"How long have you been dating Jasmine?"

"Six months," he said and she uncrossed her arms.

She held up her hand and two fingers stood up

straight in his face. "Two rooms."

He looked at me and I smiled.

"Okay," he said and she started to walk away.

"No sneaking in later, either. I am a light sleeper," she added as she continued to disappear around the corner and back towards the kitchen.

Violet laughed, as well as my other sisters, and I picked my suitcase back up.

"Come on," I said to him as I started for the stairs and he followed me.

Violet held up two fingers and I rolled my eyes. I swear it doesn't matter how old you get, your siblings are always childish when the opportunity arises, like I would sleep with him, in this house, even if we were actually dating. My mom is here. I wouldn't dream of it.

I stood in my old room and Cody stepped up behind me as I scanned it. I could not believe that my old Duran Duran posters were still up. Yes, I went through a weird 80's phase, it happens. In fact, by looking through my closet you may suspect that I never outgrew it. I smiled as he walked in and looked around.

"If I use hairspray in my hair and a little lip gloss do you think I could get lucky tonight?"

I laughed at him. "No, not unless you wear the pirate boots, that is the deal maker right there…the boots."

He smiled. "I need to go shopping."

I stared at him as he sat down on my old bed and bounced on the edge of it.

"I need you to get off of my bed, Cody."

He stood up and stared down at it.

He tapped it. "It is a little small anyway."

I grinned and walked to my window, looking out at

the two treehouses and sighed. I touched the glass and he looked past me and saw them.

"I know why you are here, Jazz."

I turned to him and the words stung a little bit. I really did not need to be reminded.

"How?"

"You told me when you were drunk. I mean, as you cried on my shoulder."

"I did not."

"You did, why is everything a situation where I have to convince you?"

I hesitated and then walked to my door. "Let me show you to *your* room."

He stared at me and decided to give up, I guess my facial expression probably told him it was best anyway. I had no need to talk to him about my dad. I was having a hard enough time accepting it myself. I walked out and he followed me until we reached the end of the hallway. I opened up the door and he looked in at all of the baby dolls on the shelves. He shook his head 'no' and I grinned.

"You get the creepy craft room."

"Great," he muttered as he stepped in and looked around. He then looked back at me and I suddenly felt bad for him.

I cleared my throat as I stared at the dolls. "This is the only spare room."

"I can handle it, I mean, come on." He walked to one of the dolls and picked it up as its eyes blinked and he dropped it. I laughed under my breath as he picked it back up and placed it on the shelf, adjusting its frilly dress.

"Just call out for an old priest and a young one if any of them start spitting pea soup at midnight."

He stared at me, wide-eyed and still creeped out, "What about midnight?"

I closed the door and stood there for a second. I heard him knock something over and I shook my head as I walked back to my room. I closed the door behind me. I sighed and rubbed my arms as I returned to the window and stared out at the treehouse.

"Two rooms," I whispered as I shook my head and smiled.

I SAT ALONE in the treehouse and stared at the maps on the walls. I had marked "safe" routes if we needed to move quickly as the zombies invaded. I smiled as I reached up and touched one of the maps and then turned as I heard Cody's voice behind me. His head was popped up in the opening on the treehouse floor.

"Safe house?" he asked me and I nodded, I had left him to deal with my mom and sisters for a couple of hours and I had to assume he was vetted to a certain degree.

He climbed in and sat down on the floor, like children do. His legs crossed and looking around the treehouse in wonder. The sun was setting and the little light it spared us showed through the cracks, one beam of sunlight was lighting up his face and his eyes. I had to admit that his eyes were my favorite thing about him. I mean, he was attractive, but my dad always mentioned eyes with people, he said they truly were the windows to the soul. I could see that Cody was pure in that way.

"Your mom sent me to get you for supper."

I looked around the room. "I guess I should go then, I mean, if I don't, she will try to climb up here and I don't need that."

"Did she do that when you were little?"

"Just once," I said and he tilted his head as I sighed and then looked at him. "My parents didn't always get along. In fact, as I grew older, the fighting was all I could say I knew about either one of them…it wasn't like that when I was little. It started when I was around thirteen and continued on until I was sixteen."

I stopped talking as memories of them flooded my mind.

"Then what happened?" he asked me.

I blinked and looked back into his eyes. "It stopped."

Cody had a look of confusion on his face. I sighed and looked down at my hands and then back up at him. "I ran away."

"Oh."

I nodded to him. "Yeah, dick move on my part, but it brought them together and after that night it all changed. I mean, I ran to the train station and I had every intention of leaving and never coming back, I didn't care. I mean, teenagers are pains in the ass anyway, I know that now, at the time I thought I was in the right. So I stood there and then suddenly the train pulled away and I found myself still here. I snuck back home and climbed up here. It was sometime later on that night that my mom climbed up here, which she never ever did, and she found me. She didn't wake me up; she curled up next to me and kept me warm. I woke up the next day with her right here. It was the one time I felt really close to her and after that night, they never fought again."

I looked up at Cody who was staring at me. His eyes a bit glassy and I tilted my head.

He spoke as if he understood. "She loves you very much. Parents are supposed to. That is their job."

I nodded to him.

"Let's go eat," he said as I smiled and followed him out and down the ladder.

WE ALL SAT around the large table that I had so many memories of. This was where we all discussed boyfriends, prom, school, gossip and so on. It was the one place we all sat as equals and shared what we wanted to say. I looked up at my mom, who took a bite of her potatoes. She was always careful to take small bites, to chew with her mouth closed and appear to have impeccable manners. I still re-member laughing at the table with my dad and spitting out food. She didn't laugh, but he did. I look back on these things now and I know she only had the best intention in mind for me. She may be harsh to some, but her manners always stayed intact in social situations. I turned to see Poppy laughing as Violet told her about her soon-to-be-ex and Rose was on her cellphone explaining why the sitter had to use the lactose free milk. Mom then stood up and spoke as everyone stopped talking altogether.

"Your dad and I had been divorced for ten years."

She sat back down and I leaned back in my chair, my mouth opened ever so slightly, as I had nothing to say. Rose dropped her phone and then picked it back up.

"I don't give a shit, I will call you later," she pressed the button and set it down. Poppy shook her head and Vio-let leaned forward.

"What?" Violet asked.

Mom took another bite as if nothing had happened at

all.

"Mama?" Rose said as Mom then looked at her.

"It is true. We divorced and he stayed here so no one would be upset. Our marriage was over years before that, but we decided to do the right thing, for you girls and keep it a secret."

"Holy shit," I said as Violet held her hand up to me and narrowed her eyes.

"You know Mama does not like cursing."

"Oh fuck it, Violet, why hold back now?" Mom said as I laughed under my breath and shook my head.

"This has to be a joke," I muttered.

"No, Jasmine, it is not. I just thought that it was time, seeing that he is gone now. I mean, really gone," she said and then she took another bite of her food.

Poppy stood up and started to cry, she was always the emotional one. She stepped back and ran up the stairs to her old room. I sat there as Cody was completely silent. I felt so bad for him. I mean, here he was doing me a weird favor and now this bullshit.

"I cannot believe this," I said as I stared at her. She set her fork down and looked at me.

"You know we were not happy Jasmine. Every one of you knew it, well minus you, of course, Cody." He nodded to her and took a drink from his glass. "We fought for years, to the point of running you away from us," she looked at me and I shook my head.

"Do not lay this on me, Mom."

"I am only telling you that after you ran away we decided to do it, for all of our sakes, and that is when I started sleeping with Marty."

"Marty the meat man?" Rose asked her as she shook

231

her head and Mom looked at her.

"Butcher, not meat man. You make it sound barbaric."

I rubbed my forehead as if I may be having a breakdown as Cody continued to drink until it was gone. He set it down and said nothing.

"So let me get this right, I ran away, then you two ended your marriage, Dad stayed here and you started boning Marty?" I said as my voice went up an octave.

Cody smiled as he looked down into his lap as Rose, Daisy and Violet looked at me.

"Really, Jazz? Boning, for Chris's sake," Rose said and I rolled my eyes.

"Oh, you can say meat man, but I can't say boning?"

"I was not being disrespectful," she said as she leaned back and I laughed.

"He was fucking that girl at the post office…. Betty, the one with the large breasts," Mom said.

"I will not, I can't listen to this stuff." Daisy finally said as she stood up. Mom looked up at her and shook her head.

"We are all adults here, Daisy."

"Really, are we?" she asked as she stormed off. I sat there feeling dizzy from the insanity of it all.

"That is two f-bombs from you, Mom, in less than 10 minutes. I may pass out," I said as Cody stood up.

"Wine?" he asked.

Everyone ignored him as he walked towards the kitchen.

"This is complete bullshit, Mom, I mean, ten years?" Violet said and Mom looked at her.

"You are getting a divorce Violet, do not try to be

condescending to me."

"Nice," Violet said as she stood up and stormed off leaving me and Rose staring at each other.

"I can't, I mean, really Mom?" Rose said as she stood up and I watched her go. Cody stepped back into the room, as it was just me and Mom now. He held the bottle up and Mom held her glass out to the side. I lifted mine too, it was time for a drink, hell, it was time for the whole damn bottle.

CHAPTER FOUR

Good Kisser

I LAY ON my bed. My feet up behind me, laying on my stomach as I had so many times before when I lived at home. I had my dad's old picture in front of me and I placed my fingers to the glass and felt it all cold to the touch. I jumped slightly as a light knock came to my door. I slid from the bed and walked to my door, opening it up to see Cody standing in the hallway. He smiled at me and waved his toothbrush at me.

"I need toothpaste."

"Oh," I said as I left my door open and walked back to my suitcase. It lay open on the floor. I did not even bother to take anything out of it. Maybe that was my way of making this go faster. I rummaged through my things until I found my toothpaste and pulled it out. I stood up and he was in my room. I held it up and smiled at him.

"Here."

He stepped up and took it from me, but he hesitated and then decided to speak. I should have known it was really not about the toothpaste with him.

"That was some heavy stuff."

I rubbed my neck and then nodded as I crossed my

arms on my chest. He grinned at me.

"You do realize you do that when you don't want to talk about something."

I relaxed and let my arms rest at my sides, all awkward.

"I don't…I mean, maybe I do. I don't know. What is with you analyzing people?"

He stood there and tapped the toothpaste on the side of his leg.

"I guess it is just a genetic thing."

I sat down on my bed and stared at him. "Genetic?"

"My mom was a psychiatrist."

I shook my head. "Great, I mean no disrespect to her, but this is the house that crazy built. You will have plenty of fun here."

He stared at me and lowered the toothbrush and paste in his hands. He walked to my bed and sat down next to me as I tried to ignore him, but he smelled amazing and I was not in my right mind.

"You know, children of divorce have a hard time connecting with people and even though they never told you, or any of your sisters, you still felt the change and it effected you, all of you."

I narrowed my eyes and turned on the bed as I stared at him.

"Listen, Cody. I get that you want to help me, I do, but I just can't do this, this thing you are trying to do with me. I know it sounds shitty and I wish that I…"

His lips pressed against my own, shutting me up as he needed to. My eyes closed and all I could think about was how soft his lips were. How good he smelled and how nice it was to feel someone this close to me. Even someone that

I did not really know. He lifted his hand and touched my face. His fingertips gently brushing against my skin. I stopped breathing as his tongue slid inside of my mouth and, for a moment, I was consumed with only thoughts of him. His eyes, his lips…how he smelled and his touch. We started to lean back and he moaned, deep in the back of his throat as I reached out and slid my hands under his shirt. His skin warm, his muscles tight and inviting me in. He suddenly stopped and leaned back from me as I opened my eyes and stared at him. He stood up and shook his head.

"Oh my God. You know what? I am sorry, that was crazy, I had no right to do that and I just…I gotta go brush my teeth and stuff, I can't…I am so sorry, Jasmine."

I was half out of breath and stood up, swaying on my feet a little bit. His kiss had made me light headed. "Cody."

He hurried out as I stood there by my bed and slowly reached up with one hand to my lips. My fingers gently touching where he had been. The traces that he left behind on me haunting me well into the night.

I SAT AT the table with a blank look on my face. Mom had insisted on breakfast for everyone and I tried to pull my "coffee only" routine, but she ignored me. Not that I was surprised at all by it. I glanced up and saw Cody sitting there, picking at his plate and I leaned up and grabbed my fork. Mom glanced at him and then to me.

"You should take Cody to see the flower garden today."

I took a breath and cut the sausage on my plate, which smelled amazing, by the way. I slipped a small piece into my mouth and chewed to avoid speaking. The kiss had thrown me, more that I needed it to. She leaned back and then continued on.

"Cody, the garden is something my family started in this town back in the early 1900's. It is a staple and has served as a beautiful spot for many a marriage ceremony, including my own and Violet's."

Violet shook her head. "Yeah, that worked out well."

"I am sorry that you are so bothered by what we did, but your dad and I felt it was the best for everyone."

"How would I know that?" she asked and then continued on as she often did when she was aggravated. "I mean, Dad is gone, he can't say anything about it, now can he?"

Mom slammed her hand on the table and everyone jumped a little bit, except for Cody. He slid some sausage into his mouth and chewed, trying to ignore it all. I leaned back and watched as Violet went into defensive mode.

"Seriously, it is not about you, Mom," She said as she stood up and my mom's eyes remained locked on hers.

"Violet, I do understand that you are not yourself because of your situation, but in my house you will treat me with respect and speak of your dad kindly, or you are welcome to go home."

Violet stood there and then sat back down very slowly. It was not something I had not seen before. Mom had often told us exactly how it would be and it was something you accepted or you were welcome to go elsewhere.

"I am sorry," she said as she looked at her plate and then she started to cry. Mom stood up and walked over to her, she placed the back of her hand to her cheek as Violet laid her own hand over Mom's. She closed her eyes and

Mom looked around the table.

"I miss him, just because we ended our marriage did not mean that I did not love him as a friend, a man who always stood by me, even in divorce, and he did give me my garden of you children. All of you named after the most beautiful flowers in the world to me. All I ever wanted was a family and he gave me that, so I never hated him, I never disrespected him, but what you need to understand is that it took two of us to do this. Two of us to create all of you and two of us to make this house a home."

I looked down and then glanced over at Cody as he watched her. His eyes glossy, as everyone's were.

"Mom, why don't you go out in your garden, we can clean up here," I said and she grinned at me. She nodded and Violet looked up at her and nodded.

"Okay, then afterward, I suggest that everyone go out and enjoy the day. Tomorrow is the funeral and it will not be easy."

She left us all sitting there in silence. Her words carried the weight needed to stop the bickering and bitterness. I felt a bit ashamed that I was worried about how I would feel being here, truth was, I felt at home, as I always had. Regardless of the fact that my sisters were different than I was, regardless of everything. It was home and Mom was right, they had provided it in abundance, even carrying on as if things were normal for our sakes.

I stood up and grabbed my plate, one by one, the rest of them did too and we all helped clear the table. Once the dishes were done, I looked at Cody. I reached out and took his hand, not afraid to show him a bit of affection and we left the house and headed for the center of town and the "garden" my mom had mentioned to us.

We stopped and looked up at the large black wrought iron gates. Green ivy wound its way through every bar, the pungent smell of flowers wafting over both of us. I closed my eyes as a cool breeze carried the sweet aroma on the wind. I felt Cody's grip tighten on my hand and I looked at him. He stared past the gates as if his memory was jolted. I spoke to him as his head quickly turned, allowing his face to light up with a beam of sunlight that rained down through the clouds.

"Cody, you don't have to stay here. I mean, I appreciate you coming with me, saving me the initial brunt of my sisters, but honestly, this is not your problem. This is my mine and I just..." He turned to me and pulled my hand up to his chest. I watched as his free hand covered our hands.

"I wouldn't dream of leaving," he said very quietly. I stared into his blue eyes. He looked sincere, as sincere as anyone could be. I parted my lips, ready to concede, but cautiously choosing my words.

"I just don't know why...why me? Why did you even come with me?"

He grinned and leaned in closer to my face. "You really suck at noticing when someone likes you, Jazz."

I blinked as the wind blew my hair up around my face and his eyes never broke their gaze on my own. I wanted so badly to lean in and feel his lips against mine again. I wanted for him to hold me close, to feel his body against me. My fingertips hummed as he leaned forward and then a familiar voice broke the moment in two.

"Jasmine?"

We both turned as I saw her walking towards me. *Her* being my first girlfriend, so to speak. We had never gone all the way, but the kissing and groping had occurred for over a year, my junior year in high school.

"Jess?" I said as I let Cody's hand go and walked up to her. She looked as beautiful as ever. Her hair, dark chocolate brown, hanging in loose natural curls over her shoulders. Her eyes a bright green, so green you would almost think that she must have contacts in, but she didn't. Her skin was pale, almost white as snow…snow white, as I often called her when we were growing up. She was gorgeous, and I certainly noticed when we were in high school. Our secret world that we had built with each other was something we never even talked about. There was no discussion and when we hit our senior year, life simply pushed us apart, but now, well, here she was, standing before me as pretty as ever. She smiled, her pinkish full lips parting as my eyes inadvertently looked at them. She grabbed me and the hug was tight and meaningful as she whispered into my ear.

"I am so, so, sorry Jazz, I heard about your dad. I just…I don't know what to say."

She held onto me and then she glanced up at Cody who was watching us very closely. She grinned and let me go, but her hands still rested on my arms.

"Thank you," I said to her as she let her eyes glance behind me and I turned and looked at Cody. I turned back to Jess and tried to smile. "That is Cody, he is…"

"Gorgeous," she whispered as she leaned in close to my face. I nodded to her as she let me go and walked to him. She extended a hand and he grinned as he took her small pale hand into his own. She shook it with more strength than he expected her to have.

"I am Jess Jarvis and you are?" she asked him as she continued to shake his hand. He stopped her and lifted her hand up to his mouth and kissed it as her eyebrow rose. She glanced back at me as I crossed my arms on my chest and shrugged my shoulders. "A gentleman, I see," she added as his lips left her hand and he smiled.

"Cody Baker."

She tilted her head, "So, Cody Baker, how long have you been with Jazz?"

He laughed as I stepped up next to her and bumped her shoulder. "She is messing with you, I am sure Jess knows the grilling my mom put you through." He looked into her eyes and then back to me.

"Well worth it." He added as he let Jess's hand go and she glanced at me.

"Where did you find him and are there anymore?" I laughed as she looked back up at him.

"I have one brother, but I have to let you down gently and just say that he is married, with children."

"Really?" I asked him as his eyes darted to mine and Jess stared at me, curious as to why I did not know that bit of information.

"Yes. He got married about five years ago, I think."

"You think?" Jess asked and he smiled at her.

"Well, we are not exactly...close."

"Ahhhh," she said as it satisfied her insatiable need to know everything. She was always like that in school, too. She was not a gossiper by trade, but a collector of information nonetheless.

"You have nice lips, I bet you are a good kisser."

"Jess," I said as I rolled my eyes. She laughed and then looked back at him.

"I am," he said, without hesitation, and I could not disagree.

"As good as me?" she asked, as she glanced at me. My cheeks reddened. Cody said nothing, but I am sure he is smart enough to understand an insinuation.

"Huh," he said as she wrapped her arm into my own and pulled me through the black gates into the center garden. Cody rubbed his neck a couple of times and then followed us, enjoying his new revelation about me and my apparent need to not mention it.\

Thank you and I do hope you enjoyed this preview of "Stardust". It will be releasing on Amazon August 17th, 2014 with Hot Ink Press. Thank you again to L.P. Dover for graciously allowing a sample of my work to be shared in her book. I do appreciate it, as always.

Xoxo ~Rue

Made in the USA
Charleston, SC
06 July 2016